Mavin had just discovered that she could change the length of her toes.

The feeling was rather but not entirely like pain. There was a kind of itchy delight in it as well, not unlike the delight which could be evoked by stroking and manipulating certain body parts, but without that restless urgency. There was something in it, as well, of the fear of falling, a kind of breathless gap at the center of things as though a misstep might bring sudden misfortune. . . .

THE SONG OF
MAVIN MANYSHAPED

SHERI S. TEPPER

ACE FANTASY BOOKS
NEW YORK

THE SONG OF MAVIN MANYSHAPED

An Ace Fantasy Book / published by arrangement with
the author

PRINTING HISTORY
Ace Original / March 1985

ISBN: 0–441–77523–3

Ace Fantasy Books are published by The Berkley Publishing Group,
200 Madison Avenue, New York, New York 10016.
PRINTED IN THE UNITED STATES OF AMERICA

THE SONG OF
MAVIN MANYSHAPED

Chapter 1

Around the inner maze of Danderbat keep—with its hidden places for the elders, its sleeping chambers, kitchens and nurseries—lay the vaster labyrinth of the outer p'natti: slything walls interrupted by square-form doors, an endless array of narrowing pillars, climbing ups and slithering downs, launch platforms so low as to require only leaping legs and others so high that wings would be the only guarantee of no injury.

Through the p'natti the shifters of all the Xhindi clans came each year at Assembly time, processions of them, stiff selves marching into the outer avenues only to melt into liquid serpentines which poured through the holes in the slything walls; into tall wands of flesh sliding through the narrowing doors; into pneumatic billows bounding over the platforms and up onto the heights; all in a flurry of wings, feathers, hides, scales, conceits and frenzies which dazzled the eyes and the senses so that the children became hysterical with it and hopped about on the citadel roof as though an act of will could force them all at once and beforetime into that Talent

1

they wanted more than any other. Every year the family Danderbat changed the p'natti; new shaped obstacles were invented; new requirements placed upon the shifting flesh which would pass through it to the inner maze, and every year at Assembly the shifters came, foaming at the outer reaches like surf, then plunging through the reefs and cliffs of the p'natti to the shore of the keep, the central place where there were none who were not shifters—save those younglings who were not sure yet what it was they were.

Among these was Mavin, a daughter of the shape-wise Xhindi, form-family of Danderbat the Old Shuffle, a girl of some twelve or fourteen years. She was a forty-season child, and expected to show something pretty soon, for shifters came to it young and she was already older than some. There were those who had begun to doubt she would ever come through the p'natti along the she-road reserved for females not yet at or through their child-bearing time. Progeny of the shifters who turned out not to have the Talent were sent away to be fostered elsewhere as soon as that lack was known, and the possibility of such a journey was beginning to be rumored for Mavin.

She had grown up as shifter children do when raised in a shifter place, full of wild images and fluttering dreams of the things she would become when her Talent flowered. As it happened, Mavin was the only girl child behind the p'natti during that decade, for Handbright Ogbone, her sister, was a full decade older and in possession of her Talent before Mavin was seven. There were boys aplenty and overmuch, some saying with voices of dire prophecy that it was a plague of males they had, but the Ogbone daughters were the only females born to be reared behind the Danderbat p'natti since Throsset of Dowes, and Throsset had fled the keep as long as four years before. Since there were no other girls, the dreams which Mavin shared were boyish dreams. Handbright no longer dreamed, or if she did, she did not speak of it.

Mavin's own mother, Abrara Ogbone, had died bearing the boy child, Mertyn—caught by the shift-devil, some said, because she had experimented with forbidden shapes while she was pregnant. No one was so heartless as to say this to Mavin directly, but she had overheard it without in the least understanding it several times during her early years. Now at an age where her own physical maturity was imminent, she understood better what they had been speaking of, but she had not yet made the jump of intuition which applied this knowledge to herself. She had a kind of stubborn naiveté about her which resisted learning some of the things which other girls got with their mother's milk. It was an Ogbone trait, though she did not know it. She had not before now understood flirting, for example, or the reasons why the men were always the winners of the processional competitions, or why Handbright so often cried in corners or was so weary and sharp-tongued. It wasn't that she could not have understood these things, but more that she was so busy apprehending everything in the world that she had not had time before to make the connections among them.

She might have been enlightened by overhearing a conversation between two hangers-on of the Old Shuffle —two of the guards cum hunters known as "the Danderbats" after Theobald Danderbat, forefather and tribal god, direct line descendent, so it was said, from Thandbar, the forefather of all shifters—who kept themselves around the keep to watch it, they said, and look after its provisioning. So much time was actually spent in the provisioning of their drinking and lechery that little enough energy was left for else.

"Everytime I flex a little, I feel eyes," Gormier

Graywing was saying. "She's everwhere. Anytime I've a mind to shift my fingers to get a better grip on something, there she is with her eyes on my hands and, like as not, her hand on mine to feel how the change goes. If there's such a thing as a' everwhere shifter child, it's this she-child, Mavin." Gormier was a virile, salacious old man thing, father of a half-dozen non-shifter whelps and three true-bred members of the clan. He ran a boneless ripple now, down from shoulders through fingers, a single tentacle wriggle before coming back to bone shape in order to explain how he felt. Some of the Danderbats would carry on whole conversations in muscle talk without ever opening their mouths. "Still, there's never a sign she knows she's female and I'm male, her not noticing she gives me a bit of tickle."

" 'Tisn't child flirtiness." The other speaker was Haribald Halfmad, so named in his years in Schlaizy Noithn and never, to his own satisfaction, renamed. "There's no sexy mockery there. Just that wide-eyed kind of oh-my look what you'd get from a baby with its first noisy toy. She hasn't changed that look since she was a nursling, and that's what's discomfiting about her. When she was a toddler, there was some wonder if she was all there in the brain net, and she was taken out to a Healer when she was six or so, just to see."

"I didn't know that! Well then, it must have been taken serious; we Old Shuffle Xhindi don't seek Healers for naught."

"We Danderbats don't seek Healers at all, Graywing, as you well know, old ox. It was her sister Handbright took her, for they're both Ogbones, daughter of Abrara Ogbone—she that has a brother up Battlefox way. But that was soon after the childer's mother died, so it was forgiven as a kind of upset, though normally the Elders would have had Handbright in a basket for it. Handbright brought her back saying the Healer found nothing wrong with the child save sadness, which would go away of itself with time. Since then the thought's been that she's a mite slow but otherwise tribal as the rest of us. I wish she'd get on with it, for I've a mind to try her soon as her Talent's set." And he licked his lips, nudging his fellow with a lubricious elbow. "If she doesn't get on with it, I may hurry things a bit."

The object of this conversation was sitting at the foot of a slything column in the p'natti, in full sight of the two old man things but as unconscious of them as though she had been on another world. Mavin had just discovered that she could change the length of her toes.

The feeling was rather but not entirely like pain. There was a kind of itchy delight in it as well, not unlike the delight which could be evoked by stroking and manipulating certain body parts, but without that restless urgency. There was something in it, as well, of the fear of falling, a kind of breathless gap at the center of things as though a misstep might bring sudden misfortune. Despite all this, Mavin went on with what she was doing, which was to grow her toes a hand's-width longer and then make them shorter again, all hidden in the shadow of her skirts. She had a horrible suspicion that this bending and extending of them might make them fall off, and in her head she could see them wriggling away like so many worms, blind and headless, burrowing themselves down into the ground at the bottom of the column, to be found there a century hence, still squirming, unmistakably Mavin's toes. After a long time of this, she brought her toes back to a length which would fit her shoes and put them on, standing up to smooth her apron and noticing for the first time the distant surveillance offered by the two granders on the citadel high porch. She made a little face, as she had seen Handbright do, remotely aware of what the two old things usually chatted about but still not making any connection between that and herself. She was off to tell Handbright about her toes, and there was room for nothing else in her head at the moment, though she knew at the edges of her consciousness the oldsters had been talking man-woman stuff.

But then everyone was into man-woman stuff that year. Some years it was fur, and some years it was feathers. Some years it was vegetable-seeming which was the fad, and other years no one cared for anything except jewels. This year was sex form changing, and it was somewhat titillating for the children, seeing their elder relatives twisting themselves into odd contorted shapes with nerve ends pushed out or tucked in in all sorts of original ways. Despite the fact that shifters had no feeling of shame over certain parts—those parts being changed day to day in suchwise that little of the original topography could still be attached to them—the younglings who had not become shifters yet were tied to old, non-shifter forebear emotions which had to do with the intimate connections between things excretory and things erotic. It could not be helped. It was in the body shape they were born with and in the language and in the old stories children were told, and in the things all children did and thought and said, ancient as apes and true as time. So the children, looking upon all this changing about, found a kind of giggly prurience in it despite the fact that they were shifter children every one, or hoped they were soon to be.

All this lewd, itchy stuff to do with man and woman made Mavin uncomfortable in a deep troublesome way. It was by no means maidenly modesty, which at one time it would have been called. It was a deeper thing than that—a feeling that something indecent was being done. The same feeling she had when she saw boys pulling the wings off zip-birds and taunting them as they flopped in the dust, trying, trying, trying to fly. It was that same sick feeling, and since it seemed to be part and parcel of being shifter, Mavin decided she wouldn't tell anyone except Handbright she was shifter, not just yet.

Instead, she smoothed her apron, pointedly ignored the speculative stares of old Graywing and Haribald, and walked around the line of slything pillars to a she-door. At noon would be a catechism class, and though Mavin made it a practice to avoid many things which went on in Danderbat keep, it was not wise to avoid those. Particularly inasmuch as Handbright was teaching it and Mavin's absence could not pass unnoticed. Since she was the only girl, it would not pass unnoticed no matter who was teaching, but she did not need to remind herself of that.

Almost everyone was there when she arrived, so she slipped into a seat at the side of the room, attracting little attention. Some of the boys were beginning to practice shifter sign, vying with one another who could grow the most hair on the backs of their hands and arms, who could give the best boneless wriggle in the manner of the Danderbats. Handbright told them once to pay attention, then struck hard at the offending arms with her rod, at which all recoiled but Tolerable Titdance, who had grown shell over his arms in the split second it had taken Handbright to hit at him. He laughed in delight, and Handbright smiled a tired little smile at him. It was always good to see a boy so quick, and she ruffled his hair and whispered in his ear to make him blush red and settle down.

"I'm nye finished with you bunch," said Handbright, making her hair stand out from her head in a tangly bush which wriggled like a million little vines. "You're all coming along in one talent or another. I have to tell you today that it looks like Leggy Bartiban will be going off to Schooltown to be fostered. Seems he's showing signs of being Tragamor. Not unexpected, eh Leggy?"

The boy ducked his head, tried to smile through what were suspiciously like tears. True, it wasn't unexpected. His father had been a Tragamor, able to move great boulders or pull down mountains by just looking at them, but it was still hard for him to accept that he must forget the shifters, forget the Danderbat citadel, go off to a strange place and become something else again when all he knew was shifter. He could take comfort from the fact that he wouldn't grieve. He wouldn't even remember a week hence when the Forgetters had done with him. Still, looking at it from this end, it must seem dreadful. Mavin ducked her head to hide her own tears, feeling for him. It could have been her. She might not have been shifter, either. No one knew she was, not yet.

"All right, childer. I'm not keeping you long today. Elder Garbat Grimsby is coming in for a minute, just to ask a few simple questions, see how you're coming. Since two of you are off to Schlaizy Noithn in the morning, he'll just review two or three little shifter things and let you all go. Sit up straight and don't go boneless at the Elder, it isn't considered polite. Remember, to show politeness to elders and honored guests, you hold your own shape hard. Keep that in mind. . . ." She broke off, turning to the door as she heard the whirring hum of something coming.

It came into the room like a huge top, spinning, full of colors and sounds, screaming its way across the room, bumping chairs away, full of its own force, circling to stop before them all and slowly, slowly, change into old Garbat, hugely satisfied with himself, fixing them all with his shifter eyes to see if they were impressed. All of them were. It was a new trick to Mavin, and when reared in a shifter stronghold those were few and seldom, with every shifter challenging every other to think of new things day on day. The Elders came infrequently out of their secret place deep within the keep,

or at least so it was said. Mavin thought that if she were
an Elder, she would be around the keep all day every
day, as a bit of rock wall, a chair, a table in some dusty
corner, watching what went on, hearing what was said.
It was this thought which kept her behavior moderately
circumspect, and she looked hard at the Elder now. He
might have been the very pillar she had sat under to shift
her toes. She shivered, crouching a little so as not to
make him look at her.

Handbright managed some words of welcome. Old
Garbat folded his hands on his fat stomach and fixed his
eyes on Janjiver. "What about you, Janjiver. You tell
me what shapes shifters can take, and when."

The boy Janjiver was a lazy lout, most thought, with
a long, strong body and a good Talent which went
largely unused. There were those who said he would
never come out of Schlaizy Noithn, and indeed there
were some young shifters who never did. If one wanted
to take the shape of a pombi or a great owl or some
other thing which could live well off the land, one might
live in Schlaizy Noithn for all one's life without turning
a hand. "A shifter worth his net," said Janjiver in his
lazy voice, "can take any shape at all. He can bulk himself up to twenty times bigger, given a little time, or
more if the shape is fairly simple. He can conserve bulk
and take shape a quarter size, though it takes practice.
The shape he cannot take is the shape of another real
person."

"And why can't he do that, Janjiver?"

"Because it's not in our nature, Elder. The wicked
Mirrormen may mock mankind but we shifters do not.
All the Danderbats back to the time of Xhindi forbid
it."

"And you, Thrillfoot. What is the shifter's honor?"

"It is a shifter's honor to brook no stay, be stopped
by no barrier, halted by no wall, enclosed by no fence.

A shifter goes where a shifter will.'' Thrillfoot threw his hair back with a toss of his head, grinning broadly. He was looking forward to Schlaizy Noithn. In the citadel he was befamilied to death, and the desire for freedom was hot in him. He rejoiced to answer, knowing it was the last answering he would do for many a year.

"And what is a shifter to the rest of the world, Janjiver?"

"A shifter to the rest of the world, Elder, is what a shifter says he is, and a shifter always says less than he is."

"Always," agreed Thrillfoot, smiling.

This was just good sense and was taught to every shifter child from the time he was weaned. The shapes a shifter could take and the shapes he would let the outside world think he could take were two different things. Shifters were too sly to let all they could do become general knowledge, for in that shiftiness lay the shifters' safety. One wouldn't look for a tree-shaped shifter if one thought shifters couldn't shift into trees. So it was that most of the world had been led to believe shifters could become pombis or fustigars or owls, and nothing much more than that. Indeed for some shifters it was true. It was possible to fall in love with a special shape and ever after be able to take only that shape besides one's true one—or for a few, only that shape forever. It had been known to happen. Shifter childer were warned about it, and those who indulged themselves by staying pombis or fustigars for a whole season or more were pointed out as horrible examples. So now in the classroom everyone nodded in agreement.

Garbat manifested himself as pleased, gave each of the boys who were off to Schlaizy Noithn a handmade Danderbat token—at which they showed considerable pleasure, intricate handmade things being the only things shifters ever bothered to carry—and then took himself away, soon followed by most of the others.

Leggy Bartiban did not go out with them. He had tears running down his cheeks openly now. "That's a shifter secret, teacher, not letting the world know what shapes we can do. How do you know for sure I won't tell all the shifter secrets when I'm gone away from you?"

"Ah, lad," Handbright came to hug him, drawing him tight into the circle of her arms. "You'll not remember. Truly. I have never lied to you, Leggy, and I'll not lie now. It is sad for you to go, and sad for us to lose you, but you will not suffer it. We have contract with the good Forgetter, Methlees of Glen, who has been our Forgetter for more seasons than anyone remembers. You'll go to her house, and the people from the school will be there, and she'll take your hand, like this, and you'll know the people, and remember them, and will forget us like a dream. And that's the way of it, Leggy, the whole way of it. You'll be a Tragamor child born, always friendly to the shifters, but not grieving over them a bit."

"Do they need to forget me my mother?" The boy was crying openly now.

"Shush. What silliness. Of course they'll not forget you your mother. You'll remember her name and face and the sound of her voice, and you'll welcome her happily to visit you at Festival. You'll see her as often as you do now, and most of the other boys at school will be the same, except for those who came to the Schoolhouses as infants and do not know their mothers at all. Now go along. Go ask anyone if that isn't so, and if anyone tells you otherwise, send them to me. Go on, now, and stop crying. I've got things to do."

Then all had gone but Mavin, who sat in her seat and was still, watching the back of Handbright's head until Handbright turned to see those keen eyes looking into her as though she had been a well of water. "Well, little sister, and you still here?"

"It was a lie, wasn't it, Handbright, about his mother?" Her voice was not accusing.

Handbright started to deny it, then stopped, fixed by that birdlike gaze. "It was and it wasn't, she-child. He will remember her name, and her face, and the sound of her voice. He'll welcome her at Festival, if she chooses to visit him. But all the detail, the little memories, the places and times surrounding the two of them will be gone, so there'll be little loving feeling left. Now that may build again, and I've seen it happen time after time."

"And you've seen the other, too. Where no one cares, after."

After a long weary silence, Handbright said, "Yes, I can't deny it, Mavin. I've seen that, too. But he doesn't see his mother now but once or twice a year, at Assembly time. So it's not such a great loss."

"So why can't he stay here, with us. I like Leggy."

"We all like him, child. But he's not shifter. He has to learn how to use his own Talent or he'll be a zip-bird with wings off, all life long, flopping in the dust and trying to fly. That'd be hateful, surely, and not something you'd wish for him?"

Mavin twirled hair around one finger, shook her head from side to side, thinking, then laid her hand upon Handbright's own and made her fingers curl bonelessly around Handbright's wrist. Handbright stiffened in acknowledgement, her face showing gladness mixed with something so like shame that Mavin did not understand it and drew her hand away.

"Lords, child! How long?"

Mavin shrugged. "A little while."

"How marvelous. Wonderful." Handbright's voice did not rejoice; it was oddly flat and without enthusi-

asm. "I have to tell the Elders so we can plan your
Talent party. . . ."

"No!" It came out firmly, a command, in a voice
almost adult. "No, Handbright. I'm not ready for you
to do that. It hasn't been long enough yet . . . to get used
to the idea. Give me . . . some time yet, please, sister.
Don't do me like Leggy, throwing me into something all
unprepared for it." She laughed, unsteadily, keeping
her eyes pleading and saying not half of the things she
was feeling.

"Well . . ." Handbright was acquiescent, doubtful,
seeming of two minds. "You know the Elders like to
know as soon as one of us shows Talent, Mavin.
They've been worried about you. I've been worried
about you. It isn't a thing one can hide for very long. As
your Talent gets stronger, any shifter will be able to
tell."

"Not hide. Not exactly. Just have time to get used to
the ideas. A few days to think about it is all. It won't
make any difference to anyone." And she saw the dull
flush mounting on Handbright's cheeks, taking this to
mean that yes, it did make a difference, but not understanding just what that difference might be.

"All right. I won't tell anyone yet. But everyone will
have to know soon. You tell me when you're ready, but
it can't be long, Mavin. Really. Not long." She leaned
forward to hug the younger girl, then turned away to the
corridor as though more deeply troubled than Mavin
could account for. Mavin remained a long time in the
room thinking of what had happened there that day.

The tears of Leggy, sent away to forget.

The words of Janjiver, in answer to the question of
the Elder, what is a shifter, to the world?

"A shifter to the rest of the world, Elder, is what a
shifter says he is, and a shifter always says less than he
is."

"I, too," she said to herself, "could be wise to follow the words of the catechism. I could say less than I am."

She went out into the day, back to the alleys of the p'natti, fairly sure that though Handbright would be upset and worried for a time, she would say nothing about Mavin's Talent until Mavin told her yes. And Mavin had begun to feel that perhaps she did not want to tell her yes. Not today. Not tomorrow. Perhaps, though she did not know why, not ever.

Chapter 2

Had it not been for the fact that Assembly time was only days away, Handbright would have worried more over Mavin, would have been more insistent that the Elders be told that Mavin had shown Talent, was indeed shifter, might now be admitted to full membership in the clan Danderbat and begin to relieve some of the endless demands made upon Handbright for the past half-dozen years. Though she was fond of Mavin—and of eight-year-old Mertyn, too, if it came to that—it did not occur to her that Mavin knew no more than Mertyn did about what would be expected of a new shifter girl by Gormier and Haribald, and by the others. Though Handbright had never told Mavin any of the facts of life of shifter girl existence, she assumed that Mavin had picked it up somewhere, perhaps as she herself had done, from another young she-person. In making the assumption, she forgot that there were no other shifter girls to have giggled with Mavin in the corners, that Handbright could have been the only source of this information unless one of the old crones had seen fit to enlighten the child, an unlikely possibility.

Indeed, if she had had time to think about it, she would have known that Mavin was as innocent as her little brother of any knowledge of what would happen when it became known she was shifter. Who could she have observed in that role except Handbright herself? Who else was there behind the p'natti to share responsibility or provide company? Had there been a dozen or so girls growing up together, as there should be in a clan the size of Danderbat, Handbright herself would have been far less weary and put upon for she would have been sought out by the old man things no more often than she could have found bearable. Part of the problem, of course, was that she had not conceived. If she had been pregnant, now, or had a child at the breast. . . . Or better yet, if she had borne three or four, then she could have gone away, have left the keep and fled to Schlaizy Noithn or out into the world. Any such realization made her uncomfortable. It was easier simply not to think of it, so she did not consider Mavin's ignorance, did not consider the matter at all except to think without thinking that with Mavin coming to a proper age, the demands on herself might be less.

When Handbright had been a forty-season child there had been others near in age. Throsset of Dowes. The twin daughters of old Gormier, Zabatine and Sambeline. At least three or four others. But the twins had soon had twin children, two sets of sons, had left them in the nursery and fled. And Throsset had simply gone, with a word to no one and no one knowing where. And all the others had had their children and gone into the world, one by one, so that for four years Handbright had been alone behind the p'natti—alone except for a few crones and homebound types who were too lazy to do else than linger in the keep, and the Danderbat granders who were there to keep watch. That was all except for peripatetic clan members who visited from time to time. Well, at least the last of the babies was now out of loincloths and into trowsies. And Mertyn was eight. And Mavin now would be available to help . . . help.

So she thought, in the back of her head, not taking time to worry it because Assembly was so near and there was so much to do. Of course more hands were assembled to do it, too, for the Danderbat were beginning to gather. The kitchens were getting hot from fires kept burning under the ovens. Foods were being brought by wagon from as far away as Zebit and Betand. All during the year shifters might eat grass in the fields or meat off the bone, but at Assembly time they wanted cookery and were even willing to hire to get it done. That was the true sign that Assembly was near, when the cooks arrived by wagon from Hawsport, all wide-eyed at being surrounded by shifters. Of course the kitchens were underground and there were guards on them from morn to night so they didn't see what non-shifters shouldn't see, but the gold they were paid was good gold and more of it than a pawnish chef might make in a season otherwise.

Mavin, aware that Handbright was distracted by all this flutter, decided it would be best to lose herself in the confusion. She knew a half-hundred places in the keep in which one might crouch or lie totally unobserved and watch what went on. Now with the Danderbat gathering from all the world, and sensible that it was a time of great change for herself whether she wished to change or no, she took to hiding herself, watching, staring, learning from a distance rather than being ever present and handy as old Gormier had noticed her being. But he was now so mightily enthralled by gossip from a hundred places in a hundred voices, so distracted by the clan members gathering in their beast-headed cloaks of fur, full of tall tales and babble, that he forgot about Mavin or any intentions he may have had toward her. Mavin, however, had merely exchanged ubiquity for invisibility, hiding herself in any available cubby to see what it was that went on as the Danderbat clansmen came home. As Gormier was a man of restless, lecherous energy, full of talk, a good one to watch if one wanted to learn things, she followed him about as she had done for years, peering down on him from odd corners above rafters or from rain spouts. It was thuswise she finally lost her stubborn naiveté.

Gormier and Haribald were helping unload a wagon of vegetables which had been hauled all the way from Zebit up the River Haws and the windy trail to the top of the table mountain on which the keep sat, just east of the range of firehills which separated it from Schlaizy Noithn. As they were about this business, they heard a drumming noise and looked out through the p'natti to see a vast brown ball, leathery hard, with arms at either edge, cudgeling itself to make a thunder roar. They set up a hail which Mavin heard, hid as she was under the edge of the keep roof in a gutter, and the drum ceased pounding upon itself to make a trial run at the p'natti. It assaulted the launching ramps, rolling upward at increasing speed, propelling itself by hand pushes along its circumference, to take projectile form as it left the ramp, then a winged form which snagged the top of a slything pillar with a hooked talon only to change again into a fluid serpent which slythed down the pillar before launching upward once more in a flurry of bright veils which floated upon the sky, the veils forming a brilliant parachute against the blue. Even Mavin gasped, and the granders made drum chests for themselves, beating with their arms, an answering thunder of applause. So the falling parachute, making itself into a neat bundle as it dropped, became a shifter man on the ground before them, the parachute veils gathering in and disappearing

into the general hard shape. Mavin recognized him then
as Wurstery Wimpole, for he had won the tournament
in a previous year and been much glorified then by the
Danderbat.

"Damfine, Wurstery. Damfine. Like that parachute
thingy, soft as down." Gormier, pounding him on his
hard shape back, shaking his hand in sudden pain as
Wurstery made a shell back there to take the blows.
"Haribald was just saying he hadn't seen veils used
so—or such a color!—in a dozen years. Amblevail
Dassnt used to do some parachute thing, but his was
pale stuff beside yours. You going to use that coming in
during procession?"

"Oh, might, might. Have another trick or two I've
been practicing. Might use them instead. Anyhow,
that's days away and there's days between! I've been
bringing myself eager cross country thinking of the
drink and the cookery and the Danderbat girls."

Gormier shook his head, sadly, Mavin peering down
on him from the height and hearing him breathe. "No
girls, Wurstery. Not a one save Handbright, and she's
tired of it. Hardly worth the effort. She doesn't make it
enjoyable. I've been at her bed this past two, three
years, and Haribald, too, seeing she's of breeding age,
but there's no good of it at all."

"You don't mean it! Only one girl shifter behind the
p'natti? Lords, lords, what are the Danderbat coming
to. Last time I was here, there were a dozen—two
dozen."

"Naa. Last time you was here was four years—twelve
seasons ago, and there weren't all that many. Throsset
was here then. And my daughters, but they were just
weaning the twins, one set each. And there was a flock
of visitors, of course, but right after Assembly they left.
After that there wasn't another girlchild behind the
p'natti save Mavin, and she's only now maybe coming

of age or maybe not. Lately the Danderbats've borne nothing but boys. Who would have thought there could be too many boys! There's talk among the Elders that the Danderbats may be done, Wurstery. Talk of that, or of bringing back the women who've gone out, whether they're willing or no . . . ''

"So howcome Handbright's stayed so long? What is she, twenty-four or so?"

"She doesn't bear. Never been pregnant once, so far as we know. One of these days, she'll give up hope and take off for Schlaizy Noithn, I doubt not. She's thought of it before, but we've discouraged her, Haribald and me." Gormier gave his head a ponderous shake at the pity of it all. "So if you're looking for female flesh, best ask a friend to shift for you, old Wurstery, or visit some other keep of some other clan, for there's naught here for you save one old girl not worth the trouble and one new one not come to it yet."

And it was in this wise that Mavin realized what Handbright's flushed face had meant and why it was that Mavin's being a shifter would make a difference. The truth of it came to her all at once, a complete picture, in vivid detail and coloring. She went inside to the privy and lost her lunch.

There was no time to steam over it then, for Wurstery had been only one of the latest batch of Danderbats who were flowing in from all directions, laughing and shouting in the Assembly rooms downstairs, drifting up and down to the cellars to see what the cooks were preparing and whether the wine was in proper supply, taking their chances on the lottery which told them off into food service crews day by day during Assembly. Mavin, no longer invisible, was hugged, kissed, hauled about by the shoulders, congratulated on her growth, questioned as to her Talent, and sent on a thousand errands. It was impossible to escape. There were eyes everywhere, Danderbats everywhere, both grown ones and childer ones, for some Danderbat shes chose to take their childer with them rather than leave them in the nurseries of the keep. And a good thing, too, thought Mavin exhaustedly as she counted their numbers and went for the twentieth time escorting a small one to the privy. It was only that night, long after darkness had come and the keep had fallen into an almost quiet that she went to find Handbright, waking her from an exhausted drowse.

"Mavin? What's wrong? What do you want?"

"Sister. I need to ask things."

"Oh, Mavin, not now! I've been standing on my own feet since before dawn, and weariness has me by the throat. You've asked questions since you were born, and I can't imagine what's left to ask!" Handbright pulled a shawl around her shoulders and sat up in her narrow bed. This room at the top of the keep was her own, seldom visited, mostly undisturbed, and it was rare for anyone, Mavin included, to come there. Handbright herself usually slept near the nurseries, and she had sought this cubby now only because there were visitors aplenty to care for the children.

Mavin, slightly ashamed but undeterred, drifted to the window of the room and looked out across the p'natti to the line of fire hills upon the western horizon. Beyond them was Schlaizy Noithn, the ground of freedom where her schoolmates had gone to try their Talent and learn their way. Of course, she ones could go there too, if they liked, after they had had a lot of childer, or when they knew they could not. This had never been important before. She had known that fact as well as she knew her own name, or the sight of Handbright's face, or the feel of a fellow shifter through a changed hide, knowing this was shifter kin even though he looked or smelled nothing like himself. But it had never really meant anything to her until now.

"Handbright, I want to go to Schlaizy Noithn." And she waited to hear the proof of all her assumptions.

"You can't do that, child. You're a she-child. Danderbat womb keepers don't go. You know that."

"Of course I know it. But I said, I want to go to Schlaizy Noithn. I want to go regardless of what the Danderbats say. Suppose I go to a Healer in the Outside and ask her to take my womb away."

"She wouldn't do it. If she did, the Elders would kill her."

"Suppose I changed me, so that I don't have a womb at all."

Handbright made the ward of evil sign, her face turning hard and wooden at the thought. Her voice was no longer kindly when she replied. "That's a disgusting thought. How could you think such a thing?"

"Ah. Well, as to that, sister, answer me this. If I have my Talent party in a day or so, or say right after Assembly, when the visitors are gone, how long before I have to do man-woman stuff with old Gormier? Or Haribald? Or maybe old Garbat himself?"

The older girl turned away, face pale. "Ah, Mavin. I don't want to talk about it. You'll learn to manage. It's part of being a shifter girl, that's all. You'll live through it. Besides, you've known all about that . . . you've known. . . ." Seeing Mavin's face, she stopped, reddening. "You *didn't* know?"

"No. I didn't know. Not until this morning. I should have known, maybe, but I didn't. I need to understand all this, Handbright. I have to know what this change is going to mean to me. Suddenly it's me the old Danderbats are leching for. Now if I'd been Tragamor, you'd have turned me over to the Forgetter to take all my memories and send me out in a minute. Wouldn't you?"

"Yes. It's necessary. We always do that."

"Even if I was a she-child Tragamor, you'd do the same. Womb or no womb, you'd turn a Tragamor she-child away to Schooltown in a minute."

Handbright nodded, stiffly, seeing where the argument was going.

"But because I'm shifter, a she-child shifter, the Elders have said I have to womb-carry for them. I can shift my legs and arms, grow fur or feathers, make me wings for my shoulders, but I can't fly or leap or turn into any other thing, for it might change womb and make it unfavorable for carrying baby shifters. If I'm biddable, though, after I've had three or four or so, or once I can't have any more, they'll let me to to Schlaizy Noithn. Or out into the world. Isn't that right?"

"You know it is. You've known those who went."

"Oh, yes. I've seen them when they went, Handbright, and I've seen them when they come back. They say Throsset fled, and there's a penalty on her if she comes back. She's gone away far, and none have seen her."

"Throsset was in love with a Demon, and he took her with him into the Western Sea. That's what's said."

"She went. That's what I mean. She didn't stay here in the keep and carry babies for the Elders."

"The word is she couldn't. She had no proper parts to do it."

"Then maybe I'm not the first to think of disposing of the proper parts," Mavin said angrily. "Handbright, remember how you used to tell me you'd shift into a great sea bird when you had your Talent? You'd be a great white bird, you said, and explore all the reaches of the western sea. You used to say that. But here you are, teaching, baby watching, cooking and carrying for the Elders, and I know for a fact that there's been much breeding done on you and no end of it planned, for I heard old Gormier talking of it and of how he'd discouraged your leaving. . . ."

The older girl turned away, face flaming, half angry, half shamed. Undaunted, Mavin went on.

"You stayed here, and let yourself be used by old Gormier, and Haribald, and I don't know how many others—and because you didn't have childer, they kept at you. And the years go by, and it gets later and later. You don't shift, you don't do processionals, you don't go to Schlaizy Noithn to learn your Talent, you don't practice, and it still gets later. And maybe it's too late to dream of becoming a great bird and going exploring, too."

"Don't you understand!" Handbright shouting at her, face red, tears flowing freely down the sides of her tired face. "I stayed because of Mertyn . . . and you. I stayed because our mother died. I stayed because there wasn't anyone *else*!" She turned, hand out, warning Mavin not to say another word, and then she was out the door and away, so much anger in her face that Mavin knew it was the keep angered her, the world, the Elders, the place, the time, not Mavin alone. And yet Mavin felt small and wicked to have put this extra hardship upon Handbright just now during Assembly, when she must be bearing so much else. Even so, she did not regret it, for now she knew the truth of it. It was a hard bit of wisdom for the day, but it came to Mavin as a better thing than the fog she had been wandering about in until the overheard conversation of the morning.

"Still," she whispered to herself, "I have doubts, Handbright. For you may have stayed out of grief for our mother, and out of care for baby Mertyn . . . and me. But there have been eight long years since then. And four long years since Throsset left. And I have been strong and able for at least four or five of those years. So why not have gone, Handbright? Why not have taken us with you? There must be some other reason.''

''Perhaps,'' said the clear voice which had spoken to her from within her own mind that morning, ''She is afraid or too tired or believes that it is her duty to stay in the Danderbat keep, oldest of the Xhindi keeps. Or because she believes she is needed here.'' Mavin left the room thoughtfully, and went down the long stairs past the childer's playground. Mertyn was there, sitting on the wall as he so often did, arms wrapped around his legs, cheek lying on his knees while he thought deep thoughts or invented things, a dark blot of shadow against the stars. Mavin considered, not for the first time, that he did not look like a shifter child. But then, Mavin had not thought of herself resembling a shifter child either and had grieved over that. Perhaps Mertyn was not and she could rejoice. She sat beside him to watch the stars prick out, darkness lying above the fireglow in the west.

''You're sad looking, Mertyn child.''

''I was thinking about Leggy Bartiban. He was teaching me to play wands and rings, and now he's gone. They took him to the Forgetter, and he's gone. If I see him again ever, he won't know me.'' The child wiped tears, snuffling against his sleeve, face already stained. She hugged him to her, smelling the fresh bread smell of him, salt sweat and clean breath.

''Ah. He may know us both, Mertyn. Handbright says they don't forget everyone. He'll know us. He'll just forget the shifter things it's better he forgets, anyhow, if he's not shifter. Why clutter up your mind with all stuff no good to it? Hmm? Besides, I can teach you to play wand-catch.''

He looked at her in surprise. ''Well if you can, why didn't you? I should've learned last year. I'm getting old fast, Mavin. Everyone says so.''

''Ah. Do you think you're getting older than I am? If

you could manage that, it would be fine, Mertyn. Then you could take me with you and we'd go travel the world.''

"I'm not catching up to you, Mavin," he said seriously. The boy had little humor in him, and she despaired sometimes that he would ever understand any of her little jokes. It upset him if she told him she had been teasing so she pretended serious regard.

"No, of course you're not. I was just wishing, thinking it would be nice to go traveling and shifting.''

"Oh, it would. If you go, you mustn't leave me all alone here, Mavin. I had Leggy, and he's gone, and there's only Handbright except you. I want to go traveling and shifting more than anything. I dream about it sometimes, when I'm asleep and when I'm awake. I want to go. But you can't go until you've had childer, Mavin. Girls aren't supposed to. Janjiver says it messes up their insides."

Mavin bit her lip, wanting to laugh at his tone of voice, unable to do so for the tears running inside her throat. "Tell me, Mertyn, why it is it doesn't mess up a boy shifter's insides? Boys have baby-making parts, too, don't they? But I've seen them shift their parts all over themselves and then put them back and make a baby the same day. So why is it only she-shifters have to be so careful?''

The boy looked doubtful, then thoughtful in that way he sometimes had. "I don't know. That would be very interesting to know, wouldn't it. What the difference is. I'll ask Gormier Graywing. . . .''

"Don't," she said harshly. "Let me find out, brother child. I'd rather." She left him sitting there under the stars, went out only to return and whisper to his shadow crouching dark against the wall, "Mertyn, if I were to figure out a way to go traveling, would you go with me?''

His voice when he replied was all child. "Oh, Mavin, could you? That would be fun!"

Could she? Could she? Could she do what Throsset of Dowes was said to have done? Leave in the dark of night, slipping away in silence, losing herself in the fire hills or the roads away north to Pfarb Durim. Oh, the mystery and wonder of Pfarb Durim, city of the ancients!

This was only dream stuff, only thoughts and ruminations, not intentions. She was not yet at the point of intention. Meantime it was Old Shuffle time, Assembly time, and she no less than any in the keep would watch the processions on the morrow.

For it was tomorrow that the visitors would come, tomorrow that the first procession would come through the p'natti, through Gormier's new pillars and doors. Even now those of the younger clans were probably roaming about in the fire hills in pombi shape or fustigar shape or flying high overhead, endlessly circling like great waroo owls, ready to assemble with first light, making themselves a great drum orchestra to beat the sun up out of bed. She went to sleep in a cubby which faced the sunrise, so that the coming of the shifters should not take her by surprise.

They began before dawn, drumming, hooting, whistling, a cacophonous hooraw which woke every person in the keep and brought them all to the roof where today's kitchen crew gave them hot spiced tea and biscuits made of ox-root, all nibbling quietly in the pre-morn darkness while out in the firehills that un-gamish hooraw went on and on, rising and falling. Mavin huddled in her blanket, perched within the rainspout once more, out of sight and therefore out of anyone's mind at all, she told herself. She did not want to see Handbright's face.

It came toward dawn, and the Elders put their score

pads on their laps, ready to note what it was they liked
about the procession, already seeing shifting shapes out
beyond the p'natti, high tossed plumes, lifted wings,
whirlings and leapings just at the edge of the light.
Mavin waited, holding her breath. She had told herself
that she was not so childish as to be excited, but the
breath stuck in her throat nonetheless.

Full light. Out at the edge of the p'natti a hedge of
prismed spears arose, shattering light in a thousand directions, then broke into shapes which came forward to
the music of their own drumming. They came low, then
upward to fly, to catch, to slide down, to rear upward
again, to sparkle in jeweled greens and blues, fiery reds
and ambers, scales like emerald and sapphire—the
mythical jewels of heaven—and eyes which glowed a
hundred shades of gold. Beyond the narrowing pillars
they thrust upward into trees of gems, glittering from a
million leaves, slid forward between the pillars and confronted the square-form portals in contracting shapes of
bulked steel, gleaming gray and shiny. Around the
slither-downs they came, erupting now into different
shapes, some winged, some coiled like leaping springs,
some vaporous as mist, all to break like water upon the
barrier of the slything walls and take the shapes of
fustigars and pombis and owls, tumbling and leaping
over the walls and the ways until they were at the walls
of the keep itself where they became whirling pools of
light and shadow, towering higher and higher, drawing
up, up, up to meet at the zenith above the keep in a
dome, a shining lattice of drawn flesh, all the time the
drumming going on and on, louder and louder, until a
crash came to make their ears fall deaf.

And in that moment the high lattice fell, drew in upon
itself like shadow to become the visitors from Bothercat
the Rude Rock and Fretowl the Dark Wood and a dozen
other Xhindi keeps, laughing outside the walls and de-

manding entrance. So was the first processional ended. Mavin sat in the high hidey hole, mouth open, so full of wonder at it that she could not wake herself from the dream.

Still there were some hundreds to be fed, and it would have taken advance planning and great determination to hide from so many. She was winkled out and set to carrying plates within the hour, and thereafter was not let alone for so much as a moment during the days or nights.

It was on the last day of Assembly that one of the Xhindi from Battlefox the Bright Day sought her, making a special thing of asking after her and begging her company for a walk in the p'natti. He told her his name was Plandybast Ogbone. "Your thalan, child. Do you know what that is?"

She looked at him mouth open. "Full brother to my mother? But she was Danderbat! Not Battlefox!"

"Oh, and yes, yes, child. True. But your grandma, her mother, was Battlefox right enough. Bore six for Battlefox, she did, before taking herself away into the deep world for time on her own. And it was there she met a scarfulous fellow called young Theobald, so it seems she told Battlefox Elders. And he got twins on her, which was your mama and me, and then she died. And young Theobald, he took the girl child and brought her back to the Danderbats knowing their deep scarcity of females, but me he kept with the Battlefoxes, reminding me frequent that I was thalan to any of her childer. He died some time back. And so I am thalan to Handbright, and to you, and to young Mertyn.

"Time ago I invited Handbright to come visit Battlefox the Bright Day, but she pled she could not leave young Mertyn. Today I asked her to bring him, and you, if she would, but these here have convinced her the walls of Danderbat keep are Xhindi gold. It seems a

slavey in Danderbat is equal to an Elder in Battlefox—
or so she believes. No, no, I lie if I say that's true, for
I've talked with her and talked with her, and it's something other than that. Something is awry with her, and
she seems unable to decide anything. She simply does
and does and tries not to think about it. Well, you know
the old saying, 'Vary thought, vary shape.' Since we do
not take the same shapes, it is silly to expect us to think
alike.'' He shook his head. ''Though, weary as she
looks, I would expect her to have accepted my invitation. Though I have a kinsman or so there who may be a
bit difficult—most particularly one kinswoman, of
whom the least said the best—she would have compan-
ions and help at Battlefox.''

"She's the only girl behind the p'natti," whispered
Mavin, so moved by this intelligence that she forgot to
be wary of telling anyone, and him a stranger man for
that. "Until she tells them about me."

So Plandybast Ogbone looked at her, and she at him,
sharing a wordless kind of sympathy which she had not
felt from any of the Danderbats. "So that's the way of
it. And when they are told about you, all the oldsters
will be at your bedroom door night on night, won't
they? Ah, surely Danderbat keep may be the oldest and
the original, but it has fallen into a nasty sort of decay.
We do not so treat our she-children at Battlefox and
would have you welcome there. Or are you too convinced that the keep walls are Xhindi gold?''

"No," she whispered. "I want out."

"Ah. Well. There's young Mertyn. He'd miss you no
doubt."

"Bring him with me," she said. "I would. Couldn't
leave him here. To hear unkind things. About me, as I
have heard about mother."

"What is it they say about my sister Abrara?''

"That she shifted forbiddens while she carried Mertyn, and died from it."

"Oh, Gamelords, what nonsense. I've known many who shifted before and during and didn't die of it, though the Healers do say the child does best which isn't shifted in the womb. This all reminds me of my other sister, Itter, going on and on about Abrara whom she never knew and knows little enough about. There are some who must find fault somewhere, among the dead if they cannot find enough among the living. Abrara died because she was never strong, shifter or no. That's the truth. They should have had a Healer for her when she was young, as they did for me, but they didn't, for the Danderbat Xhindi set themselves above Healing. Lucky I was the Battlefoxes are no such reactionary old persons, or like I'd have died, too. She should have been let alone, not made to have childer, but the Danderbats are so short of females these two generations, and she had had daughters. She should have been let alone."

"At the Old Shuffle, we are not let alone."

He looked at her seriously, walked around in a circle, as though he circled in his thoughts. "You know, child, if I took you away from Danderbat with me, there'd be fits and consternation by the Elders. Particularly since Danderbat is so short of females just now. There'd be hearings and meetings and no doubt unpleasant things for me and you both. That's if I took you. Stole you, so they'd say, like a sack of grain or a basket of ripe thrilps. If you came to me, however, at Battlefox the Bright Day, you might have a few nasty words from Itter, but I'd not send you away empty-handed or hungry. You've seen maps of the place? You know where it is?"

She stared at him, but he did not meet her eyes, merely seeking the sky with a thoughtful face as though he had said nothing at all of importance.

"Yes," she said finally in a voice as casual as his own. "I know where it is. It lies high upon the Shadow-marches, northwest of Pfarb Durim. If I came to visit you some day, you'd be glad to see me?" she offered. "More or less."

"Oh. Surely. More or less. I would be very glad to see you. And Mertyn."

"Ah," she said. "I'll remember that, my thalan, and I thank you." She turned to leave him, full of dignity, then turned to hug him briefly, smearing his face with unregarded tears. "Thank you for telling me about mother." Her gait as she left was perfectly controlled, and he looked after her, aware of a kind of envy at her composure. It was better done than he had seen from many twice her age.

~~~~~~~~ Chapter 3 ~~~~~~~~

The Assembly was concluded. The visitors left. The cooks departed in their wagon looking weary and half drunk, for they had had their own celebration when the last banquet was over. Up in the small room at the top of the tower, Handbright slept in total exhaustion, and for once the old ones were so surfeited with food and frolic that they left her alone. Mavin, watching, made sure of this. She had set herself to be Handbright's watchdog for the time Mavin remained at the keep. That would not be long. She had resolved upon it. But she was still too untried a shifter to take child Mertyn into the wide world trusting only on her own abilities to keep him safe. As the shifter children were often told, there were child markets operating in the Gameworld, and whether a child might be shifter or no, the bodies of the young were saleable.

She knew that when they went safety would depend on covert, quiet travel over many leagues, for the way to Battlefox the Bright Day lay a distance well beyond Pfarb Durim through the Shadowmarches. And covert travel would be totally dependent upon Mavin's Talent, child Mertyn having none of his own save a sensible and thoughtful disposition. Her Talent had to be tried, and exercised, and practiced. Each night when the place was still, Mavin went beyond the p'natti into the woods—a forbidden excursion—or deep into the cellars—empty now—to try what it was she could do with herself.

It took her several nights to learn to damp the pain of shifting, to subdue it so that it did not distract her from what she was attempting. She spent those nights copying herd beasts from the surrounding fields, laying her hands upon them and feeling her way into their shapes, hide first as it were, the innards coming along as a consequence of the outer form. She learned to let discomfort guide her. If there was a feeling of itchy wrongness, then she could let the miraculous net within her sort it out, reach for a kind of rightness which felt both comfortable and holdable. There were parts which were difficult. Hooves were troublesome. And horns. They had no living texture to them, and making the hard surfaces took practice. She learned the shape of her own stomach by the forms it took in shifting, the fineness and texture of her own skin, the shape and function of her own female parts, for she had determined to ignore the proscription against shifting placed upon females by the Danderbat. Reason said that if men could do it and still produce progeny, then women could do it also. And if not, then not. She would do without childer. Whatever she might do or not do, she would not end like Handbright.

Each morning she woke Handbright with a cup of tea —aware that this sudden solicitude evoked a certain suspicion—and repeated that she did not want the Elders told, not just yet. Each day Handbright would reluctantly agree, and Mavin would go to sleep for a few hours before finding some deserted place to practice in.

Day succeeded day. Gormier and Haribald were gone from the keep on a long hunting expedition, for the food storage rooms were virtually depleted. In their absence Handbright stopped insisting that the Elders must be told, and Mavin relaxed a trifle, sleeping a few more hours than she would have done otherwise.

She developed her own systems for rapid acquisition of Talent, reminding herself how quickly the babies in the nursery learned to talk once they had begun. If one spent hours every day at it, it came fast. Even the boys who began to show Talent were not usually allowed as many free hours for practice as Mavin took for herself, for they had to attend classes and spend time with the Elders listening to history tales. With the Assembly so recently over, however, everyone was tired. The Elders themselves were off in the woods in easy shapes which required no thought. The children were left to their own devices and seemed to spend endless days playing Wizards and Shifters. In a few days the keep would pull itself together to resume its usual schedule, but just now it was open and relaxed, ideal for Mavin's purposes. She thanked the Gamelords, prayed to Thandbar it would last as long as she needed, and practiced.

She knew she did not have time to learn many different things. She could not trifle with herself, learning the shape of a whirlwind or a cloud. She must take what time she had to learn a few things well, learning even those few shapes in wonder and occasional chagrin. She worked endlessly at her horse shape, believing that a boy the size of Mertyn could best be carried farthest on some ordinary, acceptable animal. Besides, horses could fight. Horses with hooves honed to razor sharpness could fight particularly well, and she spent prodigious hours rearing and wheeling herself, striking with forefeet and back ones, all in absolute silence so that no one would hear and come to investigate. She practiced gain-ing bulk, all the bulk one needed to become a horse, practiced doing it quickly and leaving it just as quickly. Taking bulk was not an easy thing. One had to absorb the extra bulk, water or grain or grass—organic things were best. Then one had to pull the net out of the extra bulk to return to one's own shape, quickly, neatly, with no agonizing tugs or caught bits of oneself lingering. It was not an easy thing, but she learned to do it well. Not knowing what she could not do, she did everything differently than other shifters would have done it, comforted herself by naming herself "Mavin Manyshaped," and did little dances of victory all alone.

She began to pay attention to other shifters, to the way she knew them, could identify them, even inside other shapes, and discovered at last a kind of organ within herself which trembled in recognition when another shifter with a similar organ was near. It was small, no bigger than a finger, but it was growing. A few days before, she would not have known it was there. Desperately, she set about shifting that organ itself, veiling it, muffling it, so that it could not betray her. She wanted to be horse, only horse, with no shifter unmasking her as anything else. The difficulty lay in the strange identifier organ, for when she muffled it directly, it was as though she had become deaf and blind, unable to walk without losing her balance. Not knowing that it was impossible—as any Elder of the Xhindi would have told her—she invented a bony plate to grow around it which allowed it to function inside her body without betraying itself outside. The plate was bulky. She could not contain it in a small shape or a narrow one, but she could do it as a horse, and the night she achieved it she slept for hours, so drowned in sleep that it was like waking from an eternity.

Waking to find that Gormier and Haribald had returned, and with them Wurstery and half a dozen

others. The hunt had been successful; the kitchen court-
yard was full of butchery, with smoky fires under the
racks of meat, drying it for storage.

And Handbright was there with great black rings
around her eyes, looking cowed and beaten, as though
she had not slept for days. "I told them," she said to
Mavin, not meeting her eyes. "I had to. I can't go on."

Mavin looked up to find Gormier's eyes upon her,
full of a gloating expectation. Ah, well. She had had
more time than she had expected. "When?" She did not
reproach Handbright. The strange identifier organ
would have betrayed her sooner or later, and what she
intended to do would be reproach enough.

"They want to have your Talent party today. They're
drawing lots who stays with you first tonight. Well, it's
time for you, Mavin. You'll live through it, though. We
all have."

"I'm sure I will. Of course I will. Don't fret. Come
with me to the kitchen and have a cup of something hot.
You look exhausted."

"They woke me in the middle of the night, the three
of them. They . . . they put . . . I . . . I had to tell them."

"Of course." Soothing, kindly, hypocritical, Mavin
led her to the kitchen. "Handbright, listen to me. I want
you to go to Battlefox keep in the Bright Day demesne.
Our thalan, Plandybast Ogbone, wants you to come.
Promise me?"

Handbright shook her head, a frantic denial.
"Mertyn. Mertyn needs me."

Mavin thought it was only habit and a weary inertia
which made Handbright speak so. "He doesn't need
you, Handbright. He's fine. The youngest child in the
nursery is five years old, and you've spent long enough
taking care of them. You should know by now you're
not going to conceive, and you'd have been long gone if
you had conceived. So you must go. There are lots of

Danderbats can come in to take care of the childer. Besides, I'll be here."

"But . . . alone. It's so hard alone . . . and Mertyn . . ."

"You did it alone. After you have some rest, you can come back and help me if you like. But I want you to go, Handbright. Either to Plandybast, or to the sea, as you once said you would do. Today." She bent all her concentration upon her sister, willed her to respond. "*Now*, Handbright."

"Now?" Hope bloomed on her face as though this had been the secret word of release; but there was a wild look in her eyes. "Now?" Mavin wondered what had happened to make the woman respond in this way. It could not be her own pleading, for she had pled before and nothing had happened. No. Something else had happened. She did not take time to worry about what it might have been.

"Now. Become a white bird, Handbright! Fly from the tallest tower. From your bedroom, up there in the heights. Nothing carried, nothing needed—to Battlefox. Or to the sea."

Handbright rose, a look almost of madness on her face, eyes darting, hands patting at herself. "Now. Mavin. Now. I'll go. Someday, I'll . . . you'll come. Mertyn's all right. He's a big boy. He'll be fine. Now." And she fled away up the stairs, Mavin close behind but unseen, as though she had been a ghost.

Clothes fell on the stone floor. Handbright stood in the window, naked. From the doorway Mavin gasped, seeing bruises and bloody stripes on the naked form which changed, shifted, wavered in outline to stand where it had stood but feathered, long neck curled on white back, beak turned toward Mavin, eyes still wild and seeking.

"Fly, sister," she commanded, fixing the maddened

eyes with her own. "Fly, Handbright. Go."

The wings unfurled slowly, the neck stretched out tentatively, cautiously, then all at once darted forward as the wings thrust down, once, twice, and the great bird launched itself into the air, falling, falling, catching itself upon those wide wings at the last possible moment to soar up, out, out, away toward the west.

Mavin found herself crying. She flung herself down on Handbright's narrow bed, aware for the first time of the basket in the corner, the ropes, the little whip carelessly thrown down upon the stones. It was a punishment basket, the only true punishment for a shifter, to be confined, close confined, unable to move, to speak, to change into any other shape. The baskets were woven in Kyquo, tightly woven, tightly lidded. And this one had been used on Handbright, or she had been threatened with it.

So. Threatened or used; what did it matter. Handbright was gone. Mavin wiped her face in a cold, unreasoning fury and without knowing how she did it, or even that she had done it, took on the very face and features of Handbright; the well known expression, the tumbled hair, the tall, slender form bent with work and abuse, the eyes dark-ringed with pain to look upon herself reflected there—Handbright's own form and face.

"Everyone knows," she whispered, "that it is impossible for a shifter to take the form of another living person. Everyone knows that it lies outside our nature, that it is forbidden. Everyone knows that. But—but, someone has done it." She smiled at herself in the mirror, a cold smile, and went slowly, with fearful anticipation, down into the smoke of the kitchen court to confront Gormier's truculent stare.

"Well?" he demanded. "She's been told there's been enough of this holding back, has she? Celebration for her this day and for me this night. I've won the draw."

And he grinned widely at her as he displayed the red-tipped stick he had drawn. "Time I had a little luck after too long of your dead body, old girl. Time we had some fresh blood behind the p'natti."

"She doesn't want a celebration." This in the very tone and substance of Handbright's own voice, dull and without emotion. "She's sick to her stomach. She's up in my room, and you can go up there, come dark, but she'll have no celebration."

"Well, and go up I will. And after me Wurstery, and after him Haribald, for that's the way it falls."

Still in Handbright's voice Mavin let her curiosity free to find the limits of the old ones' abuse. "Couldn't you have pity on her this night? Make it only one of you?"

Wurstery had overheard this from his drying rack duties and intervened to make his own demands. "We've been days in the woods, old girl. Make a nice homecoming for us. Besides, best begin as we mean to go on."

"Well then," Mavin said in Handbright's voice, "she'll have to bear it, I suppose."

"Let's hope she bears better'n you've borne, old girl." And they went back to their smoky work in a mood of general self-righteousness and satisfaction. Mavin went back into the keep, into a shadowy place, and leaned against the wall, weeping. When she had done, the Handbright shape had dropped away, and though she tried, she could not bring it back. She went to find Mertyn to tell the boy they would leave Danderbat keep that night.

She went over it with him several times, though the boy understood well enough even at first. "The horse will come to the corner of the p'natti wall farthest toward the fire hills. You'll have all your clothes and things in this sack, everything you treasure, lad,

for you'll not be back. And I will meet you on the
road. . . ."

"And I must not say anything about it to anyone," he
concluded for her, puzzled but willing. "Especially not
to any of the Danderbats."

"That's right. Especially not to the Danderbats. And
you're to wait. Even if it gets very late and scary, and
you hear owls or fustigars howling. Promise."

"Promise." He put his small hand in hers, cold but
steady. "I'll wait, Mavin. No matter how late."

She left him, trusting him. Then to the cellars for two
more of the punishment baskets, thick with dust, hardly
ever used. Except by shifters like Gormier, for Mavin
had no doubt it had been his idea—to spice things a bit.
Then to the kitchens for a sack of grain. Then to Handbright's room. She would have to be ready by dark, and
it would take that much time to gain the bulk she would
need to become a horse—to become a horse, but first to
become something else indeed, only a part of which
would resemble Mavin.

She did not know that what she was doing was impossible. She knew only that she would not rest and
could not go until Gormier and Haribald and Wurstery
knew what Handbright had known, the sureness of
pain, the tightness of confinement. And another thing.
One other thing. When they knew that, it would not
matter that there were no Danderbat girls behind the
p'natti in future.

In the deep middle of the night her horse shape came
to Mertyn, exactly where she had told him to be. She
whinnied at him, pushing at him with a soft nose, letting
him feel her ears and neck to reassure him that all was
well. He scrambled clumsily onto the low wall, and
from that to Mavin's back, the sack of possessions
balanced in a lump before him.

"Nice horse," he said doubtfully. "Are you going to take me to Mavin?"

The horse's head nodded, and the beast stepped away from the wall, into the forest which Mavin knew as few others of the keep had ever known. By dawn they would need to be leagues away, down the cliff road which led to Haws Valley and well buried in the woods which lay along the upper stretches of the River Haws. She could not let the boy know she was shifter. His mind would be open to any Demon riding along who might choose to Read him, and it was better if he simply did not know. So, there would be play acting aplenty in the hours and days to come.

They would be safe from pursuit for at least this day. The three in the tower room would not be found for hours, perhaps not for days. Each one of them had struggled, frightened half out of his wits and mad with the pain of missing vital parts of himself. Struggle had been useless. Mavin had prepared for the encounter by taking more bulk than the three of them put together, part of that bulk a Mavin-shaped piece, and the rest a huge, tentacled thing which swumbled them up and thrust them into the baskets no matter how they howled, pushing and squashing until they were forced to take the shape of the basket, without lungs or lips or eyes. Gormier had been first, arriving full of explicit, lewd instructions for the cowering girl, ready to force them upon her, only to be thrust into agonized silence by the hugeness that was Mavin. Then Wurstery, then Haribald, each coming into the dark room expecting nothing more than a bit of the usual. Well, usual they now had. Handbright's usual. They would probably live, if they were found before they starved, but they would not father any more Danderbats. A shifter might shift as he would: once that part of his self was gone, it was gone forever. He might shift him a part which looked similar,

but he would take no pleasure from it. Beneath Mertyn's drowsing form the horse shuddered, half in horror, half in satisfaction.

Now that the boy was soundly asleep, Mavin grew
tentacles again, small ones to hold him securely on her
back, and began to run. The horse shape was well and
fully practiced, constructed for fleetness with eyes that
could spy through the dark to see every hollow or bit of
broken ground. Night fled past. Behind them in the
keep a hysterical Wurstery managed a hair-thin tentacle
to lift the latch of his basket. Behind them in the keep
was consternation, fury. The Elders were summoned
out of their inner privacies by bells. "Handbright,"
they said. "It was Handbright!" No one was thinking to
look for Mavin or for Mertyn. A shifter girl only just
come to Talent could not have done this thing. It could
only possibly have been done by someone older, someone who had practiced secretly. Ah, yes, that is why she
never conceived. Surely it was Handbright. The Danderbats had only thought the creature looked like Mavin.
The room had been dark. It had been Handbright, shifting shape, desirous of protecting (protecting?) her little
sister.

Jealous, Gormier offered. Jealous that the younger
girl would get all their attention. At which there was
much clucking of agreement, save among the crones
who looked knowingly at one another but said nothing.

The Xhindi did not believe in Healers, but one was
sent for nonetheless. The three Danderbats were in too
much pain to let nature heal them. Pain and fury.

Far off to the north, the horse ran on, the boy cush-
ioned soft on its wide back, as dawn leaked milky into
the edges of the sky. She stopped, laid him down, went
off into the woods to give up bulk and clothe herself.
When she came out into the clearing, he was rubbing his
eyes, looking up at her in gladness. "Mavin. You said

you'd be here, but I thought maybe you'd forget."

She took him in her arms, glad that he could not fully see her face. "Oh, no, Mertyn," she said. "Never fear that about Mavin. Mavin does not forget."

He slept curled in her arms, as secure as though he had been in the childer's rooms at the keep, waking full of deep thoughts about the day. Mavin had brought with her a handful of the seeds of the fruit of the rainhat bush, used by the crones in the keep whenever shallow, quiet sleep was needed by someone ill or wounded. She fed half a dozen of these to Mertyn with his stewed grain, and then made him up to look like quite another boy. She had brought dye for his hair and bits of false hair to tuft his eyebrows out and a brush to make freckle spots on his clear skin. When she had done, he smiled at her in his sleep, quite content, looking utterly unlike himself. She wanted him passive, unable to take fright or betray them by recognizing someone, for they would need to travel part of the day on the Hawsport Road which led along the River Haws all the way from the far northern lands over Calihiggy Creek and down to the sea. Later, when there was time, she would explain it all and trust to his own good sense, but there was no time now for any explanation, and she dared not trust his guile.

The horse form she took was sway-backed and old, with splayed hooves which turned up at the edges. A horse ridden by an unaccompanied child might be coveted by someone stronger, but this horse could be coveted by no one. So she took bulk and changed, scooping the sack and the child onto her back with a long, temporary tentacle and holding them in place with nearly invisible ones thereafter. Then they wandered down through the woods to the road, empty in either direction. She began to plod along it, heading north, the river on her right and on both right and left, leagues away, the crumbly cliffs of Haws Valley. On that western height, well behind her, lay Danderbat keep. It was from that height that search would come, if search came, but it did not cross Mavin's mind that the search might be for Handbright.

The sway-backed horse shape was unbearable. It was inefficient and it ached. Without in the least meaning to do so, Mavin changed herself to remove the aches and make it easier to move along the road, only to come to herself with a sense of impending danger at the sounds of something coming along the road after her. A quick self check—she thought of it as a kind of patting the pockets of herself to see what she had in them—showed her a form so unnatural and strange as to have evoked immediate interest in anyone except a blind man. Hastily, and barely in time, she shifted back into the old horse form, plodded off the road and into a clump of bushes to let the travelers pass her by. She knew them for shifter the moment they came into view as dark, moving splotches against the moon-grayed loom of the forest. She even knew which shifters they were, Barfod Bartiban, thalan to Leggy Bartiban, and Torben Naffleloose. She knew them by the fustigar shapes they had taken, ones often seen in processionals at the Danderbat keep, as familiar in their way as the actual shapes of the two shifter men. The two shapes were hard run, panting, lagging feet in the dust to stir up a nose-tickling cloud. Mavin repressed a sneeze and tightened her grip on Mertyn, praying they would not see her, know her, somehow spy her out in the horse shape with the bony plate around her shifter organ.

They did not. Instead, they slowed to a dragging walk, and then into a breath-gulping halt, sagging into the dust of the road with heaving moans of exhaustion.

"No way Handbright could have come so far north lugging two younglings," panted Barfod. "So we've got to figure we're in front of her if she came north. Not that I think she did."

"Think she went west? On no more than that crone's say so?"

"Only place she ever talked of going. Beyond Schlaizy Noithn to the sea. Wanted to do a bird thingy over the ocean. Fool idea, but that's what the crone said."

"What'd she expect to do with the childer? Put them in a nest on a cliff and feed them fish?" Torben Naffleloose chuckled, hawking through the dust phlegm of his shifted throat. "Take a big bird to carry a girl the size of Mavin."

"Well now, you're forgetting Mavin had turned shifter herself. Wasn't that what all the ruckus was about?"

"Oh, well, still. A just turned shifter is useless, Barfod, useless as tits on a owl. All they do for the first half year or so is fiddle with fingers and toes. You know that."

"I remember that. Fingers, toes, and some other interesting parts, eh, Torben. Remember when you was a forty-season child? Out behind the p'natti? Hah. All the shifter boys seeing who could . . . " He paused, listening. Mavin had shifted her weight, rustling some branches. "What was that?"

"Owl, prob'ly. No shifters around. I could feel 'em if there were. No. Just night noises. Owls. Maybe a shadowman, sneaking around behind the bushes like they do. This is the kind of mild night they like, I hear. They come out and sing on nights like this. Did you ever hear 'em?"

"Oh, sure, when I was in Schlaizy Noithn. Playing flutes, playing little bells, singing like birds. There's lots of them up around the Schlaizy Noithn hills. There was one or two shifters when I was there claimed they could talk the shadowman talk. All full of babble-pabble it is, goes on and on. They'll sing for a half night, words and words, and then you ask what it was all about and get told it was shadowman talk for 'Look at the pretty moon.' Ah, well. Now that we're as far north as Handbright could have come, what's the next thing, old Barfod?''

There was a moment's silence while the two sat quiet, thinking, then Bartiban replied, ''Now I think we start off through the woods heading south again, you on one side of the road and me on the other, casting back and forth to see can we smell hide nor fang of whatever Handbright is up to. There's others gone away west, and I'm betting my coin that they find her there. She's an unpracticed female, Torben, and unpracticed females aren't up to much, as you well know. Which is why we keep 'em unpracticed, right?'' And he chuckled in a liquid gurgle before rising once more to take another, more forest ready shape. The two went off into the underbrush, and Mavin stayed silent, hardly breathing, to let them get clear of her.

So. They were seeking Handbright, a shifter burdened with two children. They were not seeking Mavin. Then so much for the horse shape, not-Mavin shape of the journey. She laid Mertyn upon the shadowed grasses and went away a little to give up the bulk she had taken, most of it, keeping some, for she wanted not to appear a child. There were child hunters, child takers in the world, and it would be better not to appear a child. Better not to appear a woman, either, for that. So. Well, first she would need to explain to Mertyn, and after that they would decide. She lay down beside him and let the night move over her like a blanket, quiet and peaceful, with no harm in it except the little harms of night-hunting birds doing away with legions of small beasties between their burrows; the slaughter of beetle by night-stalking lizard; the trickle of melody running through the forest signifying of shadowmen, shadowmen unheard for Mavin was asleep.

In the morning she woke to the child stirring in her arms, woke to a crystal, glorious morning, so full of freedom that her heart sang with it and she thought of Handbright wonderingly. How could she have waited so long? How could she have given up all this to stay prisoned within the p'natti, within the keep, prey to those old granders and their salacious whims? It was a puzzle to her. She, Mavin, would not, ever, could not, ever. She tickled Mertyn awake and fed him from their small stock of foodstuffs, knowing she would have to hunt meat for them soon, or gather road fruits, or come to some place where such things could be worked for.

"Where are we going, Mavin? You never said."

"Because I didn't have time, Mertyn. You see, you and I are running away from Danderbat keep."

"Running away! Why are we doing that? I didn't know that! You mean we can't ever go back?" The child sounded crushed, or perhaps only surprised into a sense of loss.

"You said you wanted to go traveling more than anything, Mertyn child."

"I know. I just—just thought I'd come back to Danderbat keep and tell everyone where I'd been and what I'd been doing. Like the shifters do at Assembly. Like that."

"Unlikely for us, Mertyn. We are going to Battlefox the Bright Day, high on the Shadowmarches, for there is your thalan and mine. Plandybast Ogbone." She patted the boy while he thought on this, chewing away at the tough dried meat they had brought with them.

"He was at Assembly. He gave me a thingy." The boy rummaged in a pocket, coming up at last with a tiny carving of two frogs grinning at one another on a leaf. It was the kind of intricate handwork which the shifters loved, tiny and marvelous, done with fanatical care and endless time in the long, dark hours of the keep nights of the cold season. "He told me he had brought it for Handbright, but that I looked as though I needed it. What did he mean by that, Mavin?"

"He meant that he thought you were still young enough to be tickled by it, child, and to keep it in your pocket forever. He could see that Handbright was beyond such things, beyond hope, beyond saving, perhaps. Perhaps not."

He looked questions at her, started to ask, bit his lip and did not. Mavin, sighing, took up the story. He would need to know, after all, child or not. "You see, Mertyn child," she said, "this was the way of it with Handbright. . . ." So she told him, everything, he flushing at the harsh telling of it but knowing well enough what it was she meant. Once in a while she said, "You know what that is? You understand?" to which he nodded shamefaced knowledge.

When she had done, he whispered, "You know, the boys . . . they say . . . the ones like Leggy and Janjiver . . . they say the girls like it. That's what they say. They say that the girls may say no, but they really like it."

Mavin thought a time. "Mertyn child, you like sweet cakes, don't you?"

He nodded, cocking his head at this change of subject.

"Let us suppose I put a basket of sweet cakes here, a big one, and I held your mouth open and I crumbled a cake into your mouth and pushed it down your throat with a piece of wood, the way the crones push corn down the goose's neck to fatten it, so that your throat bled and you choked and gasped, but I went on pushing the crumbled cakes down your throat until they were gone. You could not chew them, or taste them. When I was done and your throat was full of blood and you half dead from it all, I would take the stick away and laugh at you and tell you I would be back on the morrow to do it all again. Then, suppose you came crying to someone and that someone said, 'But Mertyn, you *like* sweet cakes, you really like sweet cakes. . . .' "

The boy thought of this, red-faced, eyes filling with quick tears. "Oh, Mavin. Mavin. Oh, poor Handbright. I hope she has gone far away, far away. . . ."

Mavin nodded. "Yes. She was bruised and the blood had spotted her skin, Mertyn. She had had no joy of the granders, nor they of her except the ugly joy of power and violence and the despising of women that they do. So. We have run from Danderbat keep, but they do not know that we are gone one way and Handbright another. So, we will stop going as boy and horse and go as boy and something else. For I am a shifter, Mertyn, and shift I will to keep us safe and fed and warm of nights."

"But Mavin, you are only a beginning shifter. Everyone says they are not up to much."

"Well. Perhaps they are right. So, I will not shift much. I will only be your big brother instead of your big sister, and that only so that no one disturbs us as we walk along."

"What will we do with the poor horse?" he asked gravely.

She began to laugh, then stopped herself. No. Let him go on believing there had been a horse. "I turned it loose back in the woods. It will graze there happily all the rest of its life, so we will leave it. Come, now. Let's pack all this stuff and be on our way. We have spent long enough in one spot, and it is many such spots before we come to the Shadowmarches."

She pulled him to his feet and busied him about the camp, burying the scraps and packing all the rest. Then, when she had changed herself under his wondering eyes into something not unlike herself but indisputably male, they went out onto the road to take the way north.

Chapter 4

The road was thick with dust of a soft, pinky color, powdered rose as it fluffed upward in small clouds around their feet, coating them to the knees with a blushing glow and velvety texture. At the sides of the road grew luxuriant stands of rainhat bush, the conical leaves as stiff as funnels, furry tan fruit nestling in each. The fruit was blue-fleshed and sweet beneath the furry, itchy skin, and they amused themselves as they went, spiking the fruit out without touching it and slitting the skin away to reveal the turquoise juiciness beneath. Small boys considered it great fun to hide rainhat fruit skins in one another's beds or clothing, laughing uproariously at the frenzied scratching which would ensue. Mavin warned Mertyn with a glance when she saw him furtively hiding a fingerlength of skin, and he flushed as he threw it away.

Beyond the stands of bushes to the west the forest began, first a fringing growth of yellow webwillow, then the dark conifers building gloom against the bronze red cliffs which reached upward at their left. The cliffs were crumbly piers eaten away by ages of rain and sun into angled blocks stacked far upward to the ivory rimrock where the brows of the forest peered down into the valley. To their right the river ran silver, silent, slithery as a great snake, making no murmur save at the edges where it chuckled quietly under the grassy banks, telling its own story. Small froggy things polluped into the pools as they passed. Reeds swayed as though lurkers traveled there, though nothing emerged from the green fastnesses but stalking birds, high on their stilts, peering and poking into the mire with lancelike beaks. Sun glittered, spun, wove, twisted into a fabric of light and air and shining water, and they walked as though at the center of a jewel to the muffled plopping of their own steps.

Beside the river were hayfields, few and narrow between the water and the road. Across the river were more fields, with twisty trails leading onto the high ridge where villages perched upon the rocks like roosting owls, windows staring at them as they passed. That was the Ridge of Wicking, between the River Haws and the Westfork, which lay in a great trough north of Betand. Not far ahead, to the east, the high plateau at the north end of the Ridge bulked vastly against the sky, its black stone and hard outline menacing, the bare rocky top fisting the sky like a blow. There was supposed to be a Wizard's Demesne on Blacktop, but Mavin thought it unlikely anyone would nest there save Armigers, perhaps, or other Gamesmen who flew. Dragons or Cold-drakes, perhaps. Gamesmen of that kind. There appeared to be no comfort in the place, no kindness of wood or water. She preferred it where they were and said as much to Mertyn, who sighed, hummed, trudged along the road not talking and seeming unthinking in the warm and the light.

"Elators, maybe," she mused. "Perhaps they are initiated by being taken up there on some long, climby trail, and then once they have seen the place and can remember it, they flick up onto the high rock from the far places, flick, and there they are, the place full of Elators as a thrilp is full of seeds. . . ."

"I think Seers," Mertyn offered. "It would be nice for Seers, up there, where they could really see for a thousand leagues in every direction." He hummed again, smiled up at her as though drugged, and trudged on once more. She thought that she herself must seem as drugged as he on the sunlight and the quiet, for she was in a mood of strange and marvelous contentment, so quietly peaceful that she almost missed the sound of hooves behind them on the road.

Mavin moved into the bushes at the side of the road, pulling Mertyn along with her. "Remember," she cautioned him. "I am your older brother. You may still call me Mavin, for that could be man or woman, but do not for the love of all the powers and freedom call me 'sister'." It was easy enough for her to seem male, the changes were superficial and easy; and if Mertyn did not forget, she would pass well enough. The horse sounds came on, more than one animal, and she turned at last to see what moved toward them in the morning.

They were two Tragamors, one male and one female peering through their fanged half helms, and a rough-looking man dressed in a strange garb which Mavin did not recognise. She had been told that the school in Danderbat keep was not good for much except teaching some shifterish skills and policies, and she knew that they had paid little enough attention to the Index. She wished at the moment that they had spent more time upon it, enough time at least to recognize what he might be. Not Tragamor—their fanged helms were unmistakable—therefore probably not having the Tragamor skill of moving things from a distance or tossing mountains about at will. It would probably be some complementary talent. The man was clad in skins and furs, and he had a long glass slung at his shoulder. She had barely time to look him over before the horses pulled up and the male Tragamor leaned from his saddle to hail them in a voice both unpleasant and challenging.

"Hey there, fellow. We are told there is a way into the highlands along this River. Would you know how far?"

Just as Mavin was readying herself to reply, Mertyn spoke, his childish treble firm and positive. "Just before you come to Calihiggy Creek, Gamesman, there is a trail leading back to the southeast onto the heights. Or, if you need a better road than that, there is one which goes south from Pfarb Durim to Betand, but that is many leagues to the north."

"Ah, a scholarly scut, isn't it," drawled the skin-clad man. "And where did you learn so much about the world, small one." He seemed to be struggling with his face, attempting to keep it in its frowning mold.

"I studied maps . . sir. I'm sorry, but I don't know what your title should be, Sir Gamesman. I mean no offense. . . ." Mavin looked at the boy, fascinated, for he was smiling up at the men, a kind of light in his face, and they all smiled back, kindly, with no hint of trouble.

Mavin shook herself, drew herself into the persona she had adopted and said, "Indeed, we mean no offense, Gamesmen. We are country people and see few travelers."

The skin-clad one turned his eyes from the child to Mavin, face still kindly and happy. "No offense, young man. No offense. I am an Explorer, and there are few enough of my kind among all the Gamesmen in these lands. We go into the high country in search of fabled mines, and we must find a way the wagons can come after, for why should Tragamors delve when pawns can dig? Eh?''

"Why, indeed,'' caroled Mertyn. "Well, it is more than one day's journey to the trail, Gamesmen. We wish you speedy journey and comfortable rest.'' And he smiled, and the Gamesmen smiled and rode away, and Mavin was once more trudging in the dust which had been so full of sparkling light and peace.

She shook herself. "What did you do to them?''

"Do?'' He was all innocence. "Do?''

"Do, Mertyn. When that Tragamor spoke to us first, his fanged helm practically dripped menace at us, ready to bite us up in one gulp if we did not tell him what he wanted to know. Then, in moments, in a breath, he was all kindly thalan to us both, full of good will as a new keg is of air.''

The boy frowned, seemed to concentrate. "I don't know, Mavin. It's just something that happens sometimes when I don't want people to be cross. It's nicer to be happy and contented, so I do the thing and everyone feels better.'' He stared at his feet, flushed. "I guess I make them love me.''

For a moment she did not understand what he had said. She confused it in her mind with something natural and childish he might have said. "I guess I make them love me. . . .'' What could he have meant? Some childish game? Some pretend magic? Then came a sickening combination of horror and understanding as she understood what he meant, a kind of nausea, yet with fascination in it. "Did you . . . did you do that to Handbright, Mertyn?''

He nodded guiltily. "Otherwise she would have gone away. I would have been lonely. That's the real reason she stayed, Mavin. I made her stay.''

She could not keep the words inside. They spilled out.

"I wonder if you have any idea how horrible that was for her. . . ." Her anger went away as quickly as it had come at the response she saw. The boy wept, his face flushed and red, tears flowing in a stream, his thin chest heaving with the pain of it, all at once bereft and cast down by tragedy, lost to it.

"I'm so sorry, Mavin. I'm so sorry. I didn't know, really until you told me. They said . . . they said it wasn't so bad, not really. They said women just complained to be complaining. When I saw her so sad, I should have known better, Mavin. Truly. Shall we find her and tell her? Will she forgive me?"

She was distressed at his grief, as distressed as she had been at what he had said. A child. Eight years, perhaps twenty-five seasons in all? Certainly no more than that. And yet, to have bewitched Handbright, kept her behind the p'natti to be abused, used, beaten. . . . She pulled herself together. "There, child. There. No one really expects that you should have known better. I don't myself. Handbright is gone. I told her she must go away . . . as soon as we were gone. She isn't there any more, so we needn't go back. I'm all adrift, Mertyn. I don't know what to say to you. I'm just amazed that you can do this thing. But I've never felt you do it to me, Mertyn."

"I wouldn't do it to you, Mavin. You're childer, like me. It wouldn't be fair."

"Ah. Do you know what it means, Mertyn child? It means you're probably not shifter. It means you must be Ruler, King or Prince or one of those high-up Beguilers. But you only eight years old? A twenty-four or -five season child, and showing Talent already? I've never heard of that."

"I didn't think it was Talent. I thought it was just something I could do."

"Well, that's what Talent is, boychild. That's all

Talent is, something we can do. Well.'' She looked at him in amazement, seeing that the world around them had become less shining, less marvelous, less peaceful. "You were doing it this morning.''

"Not to you. Just to me, to the world. To make it prettier for us. You know.''

"What I know, Mertyn, is that you'd better keep that thing you can do very quiet to yourself. Don't use it unless there's need. I'm worried now that those men may begin to think, there on the road, of how sweet a child you were, and thinking may lead them to more thinking, which might lead them to deciding you have a Talent. And there's a market for any child, much more a child with Talent. I worry they may start thinking and come back for us. Me they'd hit over the head and leave for dead, but you they'd sell, I think.''

He considered this, thinking it over gravely before saying, "I don't think so, Mavin. Truly. No one has ever thought it was Talent. Not in all this time. . . .''

"All this time? How long have you been doing this thing?''

"Oh, since I was a fifteen-season child, at least. I used to do it at Assembly, to the cooks, to get sweets. They didn't mind. And I did it to the shifters, too, and to the granders when I wanted something. And to Handbright.''

A fifteen-season child. Five years old. And already with a Talent seeming so natural that no one knew he had it. Mavin tried this thought in a dozen different ways, but it made no sense to her. Children did not have talent. That was one of the things that made them children. And yet here was Mertyn. Slowly, hesitantly, she moved them on their way. "It will still be best to use it only when we must. Elsewise you may do some unconsidered damage with it. So. Agreed?''

He nodded at her, rather wanly, and they went on

their way, Mavin cautioning herself the while. "He is only a child. Because he seems to have this Talent, you will begin to think that he is more than a child, that he understands more than a child can understand. You will make demands upon him, you will expect things from him. He will make childish mistakes, and you will blame him. Don't do it, Mavin. He is child, only child, and that is quite enough for the time being. Let him live with his thalan, Plandybast, at least for a little time. Let him not have to *make* people love him. . . ." Shaking her head the while, impressing it upon herself, demanding that she remember. The light had gone out of the day, and she longed for it, longed to have Mertyn bring it back, but would not allow him to do it even if he would. "Child," she said to herself yet again. "A child." She had the feeling that she herself had never been a child, having to remind herself what she had been until the past few days. Before the Assembly she had been a child. Before she overheard the granders she had been a child. Before she had seen Handbright's body striped with the whip, before she had known what it would be not to be a child. . . .

"Don't worry, Mavin," he whispered to her. "It's really a good thing to have. You'll see. I'll only use it to help us."

They went on toward the north for that day and most of the day following. The latter part of that day they accepted a ride on a farm wagon hauling hay from the fields along the river to the campground at Calihiggy Creek. Mavin had grown used to her boyish shape, had managed to hold it constant even while sleeping. Mertyn nagged at her from time to time. "I thought shifters couldn't take other people shapes, Mavin. They taught us that. Handbright taught us that."

To which she replied variously, as the mood struck her. "I think most shifters can't," or "It was a lie," or

"I think it's only other real people we can't shift into," knowing that this last was as much a lie, at least, as any other thing he had been told.

"You need a fur cloak," he said seriously to her. "With a beast head. Barfod had one with a great wide head on it, he said it was a monstrous creature from the north. I like pombi heads best. Let's get you one of those."

"Mertyn, child, I don't want anyone to know I am shifter. I don't want anyone to know that either one of us are anything except—just people."

"Pawns?" he asked in a disgusted voice.

"Well, maybe not pawns. But whatever is next to pawns that would make the least problems. I don't want anyone carrying tales about us back to Danderbat keep. I don't want any child stealers coming after you. I don't want any woman stealers to be taking me. So, we're just two—whats?"

He began to think about this, laying himself back in the haywagon and staring at the sky. It was growing toward evening, and the lights of the campground were showing far ahead of them on the road. "I know," he whispered to her at last. "You shall be a servant to a Wizard. No one wants to upset a Wizard or trifle with a Wizard's man. I shall be the Wizard's thalan, son to his sister. That way no one will trifle with me either."

She considered it. It had a certain audacious simplicity which was attractive. "Which Wizard? We'd have to say which Wizard?"

"It couldn't be a real one with a Demesne around here, or we might get caught. I heard of one. There's one called Hagglefree who has a Desmesne along the River Dourt."

"You know some very strange things," she said.

"There are lots of old books and maps at the keep that no one paid any attention to," he replied. "We should have learned all about them at school. Someone must have learned about them long ago, or they wouldn't have been there."

"We had become decadent," she said. "That's what Plandybast said to someone at the last dinner. That Danderbat keep was decadent. That we hadn't any juice anymore."

He nodded solemnly. "So. If he's still alive, Haggle-free, I mean, then we should be all right."

"If he had a sister. If she had a boy. If he keeps servants, for some do not. We might be better to make up a name, Mertyn. Make one up."

He thought for a moment, said, "The Wizard Himaggery. That's who we are connected with."

"And where is his Demesne?"

"Ah . . . let's see. His Demesne is down the middle river somewhere, toward the southern seas. There's lots of blank space on the maps down there. No one knows what's there, really." He put his hand in hers, "Shall we swear it, Mavin? Shall it be our Game?"

"Let it be our game, brother. The campground is ahead, and we will see how it sits with the people there when I buy us supper and a bed."

"Do you have money, Mavin? I brought a little. I didn't have much."

"I didn't have much either, brother boy, but I took some from the cooks' cache before they left. It will get us to Battlefox the Bright Day—if we are careful."

The wagon driver leaned back toward them, gesturing toward the firelights down the road. "That the place you were going, young sirs? There it is. Calihiggy Campground. I'll take the wagon no further, for I've no mind to have my hay stolen during the dark hours. I'll sell it to the campmaster come morning."

They thanked him and left him, then wandered out of the gloaming into the firelight before a half hundred pairs of eyes, both curious and incurious.

It was the first time Mavin had been anywhere outside the keep of the Danderbats where she had needed to speak, bargain, purchase, seem a traveler more widely experienced than in fact she was. She did it rather creditably, she thought, then noticed that the man to whom she spoke smiled frequently at Mertyn with a glazed expression. Shaking her head ruefully, she accepted the bedding she was offered and allowed them to be guided to a tent pitched near the western edge of the ground, near Calihiggy Creek and a distance from the privies.

"I thought I told you not to do that," she hissed.

"I had to," he said sulkily. "The man was beginning to think you were a runaway pawn from some Desmesne or other. You stuttered."

"Well. I haven't practiced this."

"You've got to seem very sure of yourself," he said. "If you seem very sure of yourself, everyone believes you. If you stutter or worry, then everyone else begins to stutter and worry inside their heads."

"I thought you had Ruler Talent, not Demon Talent to go reading what's in people's heads."

"It isn't like that. I can just feel it is all. Anyhow, it didn't hurt anything. Now you've got to practice walking as though you knew just where you were going, and when you talk, do it slowly. As though you didn't care whether you talked or not. And don't smile, until they do. I'm tired. What did you get us to eat?"

"I got hot meat pies, three of them, and some fruit. You can have thrilps or rainhat berries."

He had both, and two of the pies. Mavin contented herself with one. They weren't bad. Evidently some family from a little village along the road brought a wagonload of them to the camp every day or so, and the campmaster heated them in his own oven. When they had done, they wandered a bit through the camp, trying to identify all the Gamesmen they saw, and then went back to their tent. "No one is looking for us," Mavin said. "No one at all. They've all gone back to Danderbat keep. And likely we will not see Handbright again until we come to Battlefox. Well, it's less adventurous than I'd thought."

"It's adventurous enough," the child responded, voice half dazed with sleep. "Enough. Lie down, Mavin."

She sat down, then lay down, then pulled the blankets up to her chin. They were only three days away from the place she had lived all her life, and already the memory of it was beginning to dim and fade. She was no longer very angry, she realized in a kind of panic. The anger had fueled her all this way, and now it was dwindled, lost somewhere in the leagues they had traveled. Something else would have to take its place.

She thought about this, but not long before the dark crawled into her head and made everything quiet there.

When morning came, she went out into it, telling herself what Mertyn had told her the night before. She watched how the men of the camp walked, and walked as they did, watched their faces as they talked and made her face take the same expression. She went first to the campmaster to ask whether he knew of a wagon going to Pfarb Durim, following his laconic directions to a large encampment among the trees in the river bottom. There she confronted a dozen faces neither hostile nor welcoming and had to take tight control in order that her voice not tremble.

"I greet you, Gamesmen," she began, safely enough, for there were a good many Gamesdresses in the group. "My young charge and I travel toward Pfarb Durim. Our mounts were lost in a storm in the mountains through which we have come, and we seek transport and company for the remaining way.''

There was among the group a gray-headed one, still strong and virile-looking, but with something sad and questioning about his face. He looked up from his plate —for they were all occupied with breakfast—and said, ''As do we all, young man. You have not told us who you are?'' He set his plate down beside him, the motion leading Mavin's eyes to the spot, and she saw a Seer's gauze mask lying there, the moth wings painted upon it bright in the morning light.

''Sir Seer.'' She bowed. ''I am servant of one Wizard, Himaggery of the Wetlands and I have in my care thalan to the Wizard, the child Mertyn.''

''So. Would you have us escort you against future favors from your Wizardly master? Can you bargain on his behalf?'' This was shrewdly said, as though he tested her, but Mavin was equal to this.

''Indeed no, sir. He would have me in . . . have my head off me if I pretended such a thing. I ask only such assistance as my master's purse will bear, such part of it as he entrusts to me.'' She felt a small hand creep into her own, and realized that Mertyn had come up beside her. A quick glance showed that he was simply standing there, very quietly, with a trusting expression on his face.

''Ah.'' The Seer seemed to think this over. He had a knotty face, a strong face, but with a kind of strangeness in it as though it were hard for him to decide what expression that face would wear. His hair was a little long, thrust back over his ears in white wings, and he had laid the cloak of the Seer aside to sit in his shirt and vest. The others around the fire watched him, made no effort to offer any suggestion. These were mostly young men, no more than nineteen or twenty, with a few among them obviously servants. The horses at the picket line were blanketed in crimson and black, obviously the colors of some high Demesne around which Gamesmen gathered. At last one of the young men walked over to them to stand an arm's-length from Mavin and look her over from toe to head, his own head cocked and his expression curious and friendly.

"Windlow, our teacher, does not make up his mind in any sudden way. You still have not told him who you are—your name."

"His name is Mavin," said Mertyn in his most child-like voice. "He is very nice, and you would like him very much."

"My name is Mavin," she agreed, bowing, and pinching Mertyn's arm a good tweak as she did so. "A harmless person, offering no Game." She glared at Mertyn covertly.

The man who had been named Windlow spoke again from the fire. "There is always Game, youngster. The very bunwits play, and the flitchhawks in the air. There is no owl without his game, nor any fustigar. You cannot live and offer no game."

"He means . . ." began Mertyn.

"I meant," she said firmly, "that I seek only transport, sirs. Nothing more."

"Surely we can accommodate them, Windlow?" the young man said. "After all, we're going there. And we have extra horses. And neither of them weighs enough for a horse to notice, even if we had to carry them double."

"Oh, ah," said Windlow. "It isn't the horses, Twizzledale. It's the vision. Concerning these—this. I had it the moment they walked into view. Curious. It seems to have nothing at all to do with anything happening soon, or even for quite a while. And it wasn't this one at all"—he pointed to Mavin—"but what seemed to be his sister. Looked very much like his sister. And this child grown up and teaching school somewhere. Most unlikely. But you were in it, too, Twizzledale, and you didn't seem unhappy about it, so one can only hope it is for the best."

The young man laughed and turned back to offer his hand, which Mavin took in her own, grasping it with as manish a pressure as she could, so that he winced and shook his own in pretended pain. "So. Then it is settled. You will come with us the day or two to Pfarb Durim. I am Fon Twizzledale, like to be, so they tell me, Wizardly in persuasion. Yon is Prince Valdon Duymit, thalan of High King Prionde of the High Demesne. Our teacher, Seer Windlow, you have met. These are our people, all as kindly in intent as you yourself claim to be. Welcome, and will you join us for breakfast?"

Mertyn let his childish treble soar in enthusiasm. "Oh, yes sirs. I am very tired of smoky meat." And more quietly to Fon Twizzledale, "Did he truly have a vision about us?"

"He truly did," the young man asserted, "if he said he did. I have never known Windlow to say anything which is not strictly and literally true."

"I thank you for your kindness," Mavin interjected, "but you have not yet told me what price you place upon your company."

Windlow shook his gray head impatiently, as though the idea were one which did not matter and distracted him from some other idea which did matter. "Oh, come along, come along. There is no payment necessary. The Fon is quite right. We have extra mounts, and neither of you appears to be a glutton. Have you eaten? Did they say they had eaten?" he appealed to Prince Valdon, saturnine in his dress of red and black.

That one's mouth twisted in a prideful sneer of distaste. "The child seems ready to eat, Gamesmaster. Children usually are, if I remember rightly."

"Yes, please," said Mertyn, casting his grave smile at

Valdon's face, on his best behavior, edging away from Mavin's clutching fingers toward the Seer. "I would like some of whatever you are having. It smells very good."

The Seer's face lightened, an expression of surprising sweetness which drove away the slightly peevish expression of concentration he had worn since they had walked into the camp. Mavin thought, "He was having a vision, but he couldn't quite get it, and it was like a dream he was fishing for. Now it is gone." In which she was quite correct, for Windlow had had a vivid flash of Seeing somehow wrapped around the two of them, but it had eluded him like a slippery fish in the stream of his thoughts. Now it was gone, and he turned from it almost in relief. Too often the Seeings were of future terror and pain.

"Well, come fill a bowl, then," he said to Mertyn. "And tell your sister—no. No. How stupid of me. Tell your . . . cicerone to join us, too." He turned to Mavin. "Forgive me, young sir. Sometimes vision and reality confuse themselves and I am not certain what I have seen and am seeing. I seemed to see the boy's sister. . . ."

Mavin bowed slightly, face carefully calm. Across the fire she could see Twizzledale's face fixed on her own, an expression of bemusement there, of thoughtful calculation. "No forgiveness necessary," she said. "The boy's sister is far from here." And that, she thought, is very true. She accepted a bowl of the food. It was indeed very savory smelling.

"My good servant, Jonathan Went, that scowling old fellow over there by the wagon, saves all the bones from the bunwits whenever we have a feast. I'm talking about you, Jonathan! Well, he saves the bones and cooks them up into a marvelous broth with onions and lovely little bulblets from the tuleeky plant and bits of this and that. Then he uses the broth to cook our morning grain, and sometimes he puts eggs and bits of zeller bacon into it as well. Remarkable. Then we are all very complimentary and cheerful, and he goes over by the wagon and pretends he does not hear us. Modest fellow. The best cook between here and the High Demesne. King Prionde himself made the fellow an offer, but he would not leave me and the King was kind enough not to press the matter. Ah. Good, isn't it?''

"Very," gasped Mertyn, his mouth full.

"It is delicious," agreed Mavin. The grain was tender, rich with broth and bunwit fat, and she could taste wood mushrooms in it as well. She sighed, for the moment heavily content. Across the fire Fon Twizzle-dale stared at her, his head cocked to one side. Farther away the proud Prince sat looking toward her but across her shoulder as though she did not exist, his small crown glittering in the early sun. She found herself liking the one, wary of the other. "Careful," she warned herself. "There was a time you liked old Graywing, too."

The meal was soon done. In her role of servant, Mavin moved to help those who were packing the wagons and loading the pack animals. There were indeed many extra mounts, and she found herself atop one of them with no very clear idea what to do next. Being a horse and riding a horse were two different things, but she kept her face impassive and paid careful attention to those around her. With Mertyn on the pad before her she clucked to the horse as others around her were doing, and it moved off after them, head nodding in time to its steps in an appearance of bored colloquy. Mertyn leaned comfortably against her and whispered, "You won't need to do anything, Mavin. This horse will follow that one's tail. I heard some of the visitors talking at Assembly time, too. About riding horses, I mean. They say you're supposed to hold on with your legs. Can you hold on with your legs?"

"Brother mine," she whispered in return, "remember that I am the well schooled servant—upper servant—of a Wizard. Of course I can ride a horse. Didn't you tell me I can do anything I think I can?"

He giggled, then lapsed into silence, rolling his head from side to side on her chest to see the country they were traveling through.

Calihiggy Creek was a sizeable flow, emptying into the River Haws at the conjunction of two valleys, the narrow north-south one of the Haws, the wide, desolate east-west one of the Creek. Here the waters had cut deep ravines into the flat valley bottom so that the water flowed deep below the surface of the soil. What plants grew there were dry and dusty looking, more suited to a desert than a river valley, though at the edges of the cliffs there were scattered groves of dark trees. They clattered briefly over a long wooden bridge, high above the Haws.

"Why is it so high up?" Mertyn wanted to know.

The Fon had ridden alongside and answered him promptly. "Are they not built so high in your country? Here is it built high to escape the spring rains which come in flood down those barren gullies. The water is so low now that we might have waded over, as it always is at the turn of the seasons, but when the spring rains come it will be a muddy flood once more. I have seen it almost at the floor of such bridges after the rains." He adjusted the flowing sleeve of his Wizardly robe, burnishing the embroidered stars at the cuff with a quick rub and breath from his lips.

Mertyn, remembering that he was supposed to be thalan of a Wizard of the Wetlands, very sensibly shut his mouth and merely smiled his understanding.

"Why do you go to Pfarb Durim?" the Fon went on. "Does the Wizard travel there?"

Mavin had been prepared for this question. "We are

to await further instructions in Pfarb Durim. Young Mertyn has been visiting his mother.''

"Ah," said the Fon. Mavin had the distinct impression that he did not believe her. "A very small entourage for a Wizard's thalan. If the boy were my thalan, I would not send him so little accompanied."

"Mavin is quite enough," said Mertyn in a firm voice. "It isn't nice for you to say he isn't. Besides, what is a Fon, anyhow?"

"Sorry," laughed Twizzledale. "I withdraw my comment, young sir. As for *Fon*, it is only a word used in my southernish Demesne for eldest-important-offspring. It means I will inherit certain treasures and lands held by my family and learn if I can hold them in my turn. Good travel to us all." And with that he was off at top speed, raising the rosy dust in a great cloud as he sped past the other riders and dwindled away on the northern road between the two lines of cliffs, Prince Valdon in pursuit.

Now the Seer Windlow was riding beside them, his gauze mask draped on the saddle before him, casually picking his teeth with a bit of wood. "A bit along the road here," he remarked, "where the woods begin to thicken once again, we will need to climb the cliffs. If we stay on this road along the valley it will take us to the place called Poffle, below Pfarb Durim, and it is my understanding that one would do well to avoid the place."

"Why is that, sir?" Mavin asked politely.

"Ah, well, the place has a bad name. Said to be a den of Ghouls. Old Blourbast rules there, and he is not a Gamesman others speak of with friendship."

"Is that the place called Hell's Maw?" piped Mertyn. "I saw it on a map."

"Shhhh, my boy. Not a name which is generally spoken aloud. However, yes. You're right. People speak of Poffle, but they mean Hell's Maw. At any rate, it will not matter. We will not come near the place except to look down on it from the walls of Pfarb Durim, for it lies in the chasm below those walls, shut away from light and sun as it properly should be if all that is said of it is even half true.

"I heard you say to Twizzledale you will be met in the city. I think that is well. Travel is safer in larger numbers. Not that you are not fully competent, I'm sure. Merely that . . . well, you are young." He smiled to take the sting from what he said. "Forgive my mentioning it. If you are like most young men, you hate having it mentioned."

Mavin could not help laughing. "I hate having it mentioned. Yes. Perhaps . . . " She paused a moment before going on, "it is because young people are not that sure they are competent."

"There is always that," agreed the Seer. "But that feeling does not necessarily diminish with age. It is merely challenged less frequently. When one has over sixty years, as I do, then the world assumes we would not have survived without competence. With someone your age, it could always be sheer luck." He patted Mavin's arm and nodded at her. Mavin soberly thought it over. Next time she shifted, it would be into something more bulky and older-looking. Why tempt fate?

"May I ask why your group travels to Pfarb Durim, Sir Seer? Do I understand you are Gamesmaster to the young men in your party?"

"Ah, well yes, in a manner of speaking. At the moment I am sworn to the High King, Prionde, he of the High Demesne away south in the mountains near the high lakes of Tarnoch. Prince Valdon Duymit is son of Valearn Duymit, full sister to the King, therefore thalan to the King. The boy riding off there to the left is his full brother, Boldery Duymit. We call him Boldery the Brash, for his thirty seasons have been full of troubles as a cage of thrilpats. You have met the Fon, offspring of some great Demesne away south where I have never traveled though I would much like to go. He says he is a Wizard, and one does not ask too many questions of Wizards, as you know. I am inclined to believe much of what he says although he is given to flowery passages and glittering nothings. A good boy, though. I like him.

"There are two other young men awaiting our group in Pfarb Durim, thalani of Demesnes to the north and west high in the Shadowmarches, and a youngster named Huld whose schooling has been arranged through negotiators with the King. I know nothing about him save that he shows early signs of becoming a Demon. Well, when we have all the students there, we will swing down through Betand—Betand? Yes. That is where the Strange Monuments are. You know of the Monuments? Ah. One of the wonders, so it is said, of the world. No one knows who built them or what their purpose is. Some hint that they were not built by men at all. Well, then we go on to the south picking up another student in Vestertown and then up into the mountains to the High Demesne to my newly built school. A small school. Only a dozen young men and a few boys. The young men have mostly shown Talent already, so much of the confusion and exasperation of teaching is eliminated thereby. I remember . . . seem to remember my own schooldays. What a time, wondering whether there would be any Talent at all, wondering whether it might be some horrible kind one would rather not have, some Ghoulishness or other. . . . Though, come to think of it, I have never known one who would be repelled by Ghoulishness to receive that Talent. It is almost as if our Talents prepare us for their coming. Well, all that is of no import. It will be a small school, as I said, mostly for the benefit of the King's thalani with a few others to keep them company. This trip to Pfarb Durim is likely one of the last few I will make."

All of this was explained in a slow, ruminative fashion which Mavin could hear with half her attention while her busy mind attended to the road and the river and the canyon at either side. Valdon and Twizzledale were still far ahead, Boldery the Brash riding back from time to time to inspect the face of the sleeping Mertyn and inquire whether they might ride and play together, at which Windlow shook his gray head and warned him away. "Let the boy sleep, Boldery. Time enough for your games when he wakes. Likely he slept little enough last night. Campground beds are hard as stone." Then, to Mavin, "It would probably do your charge good to have some boyish company, even of such mischievous kind as this. I have no doubt they will be deep into trouble before supper." And he nodded to himself as if in considerable satisfaction at this prediction.

The canyon walls, which had been close upon their right, began to retreat into the east; they had come to a widening of the river bottom, and fields began to appear once more between the river and the cliffs to the east of the river even as the cliffs drew closer to the river on the west. Boldery came riding back toward them in a cloud of pink, his face and short cloak liberally dusted, only his eyes shining at them in the rosy fog. "The trail to the top is only a little way on. Valdon says we need not take it. There is a road between Poffle and Pfarb Durim we can pick up beneath the walls of the city. . . ."

"No," Windlow said firmly. "We do not wish to approach . . . Poffle . . . so closely. We have allowed time for the extra leagues, and we are not short of either energy or provisions."

"But Valdon says . . . "

"I am Gamesmaster here, Boldery. We know that Valdon seeks adventure, always, believing that the name of the High King is enough to protect him. It may not always be so. The Ghoul Blourbast holds . . . Poffle. He may care little for the High King.''

''Everyone fears the name of the High King,'' the boy asserted, flushed skin showing through the pink dust.

''Not everyone, lad.'' Windlow patted him gently. ''I mean no disrespect to your thalan to say so. You have not been so far from the High Demesne before or you would know. If you think I am telling you fibs, then go ask Twizzledale. He will tell you aright, for he has traveled far enough to know that what I say is the truth.''

''Valdon says he's a pawnish churl, no Wizard at all.''

''If Valdon said that, then Valdon was either silly or drunk.'' Windlow's voice held anger, and the boy flushed again as he turned away.

''He was drunk, Gamesmaster. He would be angry I told you. Please don't tell him.''

''I won't mention it. You might remember it, however. It is never wise to drink so much that you say things others remember to your discredit. Now—ride on back to the young Gamesmen and tell them we take the cliff trail.''

Mavin had been somewhat embarrassed by this interchange, not knowing where to look, whether to seem interested or not to notice, though it would have been impossible not to hear. Windlow shook his head as the boy rode away. ''Do not attach too much importance to that, Mavin. The boy worships his older brother, as is often the case. The brother is not worthy of such worship, as is also often the case. Valdon is prideful. Over prideful. It would have been better had he not known since childhood that he would be a Prince.''

''Known since childhood?'' She was startled. ''How could anyone know in childhood what Talent they would manifest later? Why even in . . . the places I have been, they have not . . . " Her voice trailed away into betraying silence. She had almost spoken of Danderbat keep.

"I will tell you," he said, seeming not to notice her confusion. "Prionde, when he was no older than Valdon is now, took his own full sister to wife, she being Queen in her own right and talent. My studies of history lead me to believe that such breeding is often unwise. It is true that traits—perhaps Talents—are intensified by such breeding. It is also true that dangerous and deadly tendencies are also intensified. There is a certain rashness in Prionde and in his sister-wife, Valearn, as well. It is amplified, greatly, in both Valdon and Boldery. I fear for them sometimes."

"And so, the King was sure his children—his thalani would have the Talent of Ruling, Beguilement?" Within her arms she felt Mertyn stir and knew that he had heard the conversation. "He knew it when they were children and let them know it?"

"He was so sure that if they had not, I think he would have sent them away and not have seen them ever again."

Mavin gulped, possessed by a frantic curiosity which she did not attempt to find reason for. "What did she think about it. Her. His sister?"

"She has not spoken of it in the High Demesne. She seemed to like her life well enough. However, she had complained of illness since bearing Boldery, and the Healers have been unable to cure her. Which makes me believe it is not her body which ails her." He fell silent, biting his lip, then adopted a more casual tone. "Well, what a conversation to be holding with a casual acquaintance. I would appreciate it if you did not repeat what I have said. I am a loquacious old man, and on occasion I forget myself."

Mavin nodded her agreement, feeling Mertyn tense

against her, then relax. A shout from close ahead drew their eyes forward, and there at the beginning of the cliff trail Twizzledale waited for them. One of the wagons had already turned behind him and was lurching upward on the narrow way.

"We cannot get by the wagon," he called. "The way is too narrow. Shall we have tea to give them time to get to the top?" His laughing eyes met Mavin's. She flushed and looked away, though she did not know why.

From between her arms Mertyn spoke calmly, his shrill voice carrying over the sound of hooves and wheels. "Thank you, Wizard, sir. I am very thirsty. Besides, I have to get off this horse."

And as Mavin followed him to the ground she thought that she, too, had to get off the horse. The world seemed to move beneath her feet, and she was hard put to it to seem balanced and secure upon her legs. Still, she managed a manly smile of thanks for Twizzledale's hand and a cheerful offer to collect some wood along the slope to make them a fire. Once away from them all, she sighed deeply and let her face sag into its own girlish shape, just for a moment, just to know who and what she was. This role-playing demanded more of her than she had guessed it might, and the strain of it tugged at her muscles, tugged at the shifter net within her, making concentration difficult. She breathed deeply, heard Mertyn call, "Mavin? Where are you?" and managed to find both an armload of wood and a feeling of calm before she walked back toward the group, waving to the child with one hand.

Chapter 5

They came to the city of Pfarb Durim at noon of the day following, for they had lingered on the road to investigate the Strange Monuments which the Seer Windlow had longed to see. The wagons had taken some time to get up the narrow path, and Valdon had been throwing unpleasant glances at the Seer long before the way was clear, sprinkling his displeasure with remarks made just loudly enough to be heard concerning the width and smoothness of the road along the valley floor. Perhaps Windlow did not hear them, but at the least he gave no evidence of hearing the sneering remarks, and when the trail to the highlands was clear, they made their way upward in some appearance of amity. The first of the Monuments stood over the road within spitting distance as they came over the lip of the cliffs, and from that time on the journey was one of continual expostulation and wonder.

"I had no idea they were this close to Pfarb Durim," marveled Windlow. "I had always thought they were further south, nearer Betand. Though, as I think of it, some of the authorities—if any are to be considered authorities on such subjects as this—have said that these Monuments have a strange tendency to wander, seeming first nearer and then farther away.''

"Oh, come, Gamesmaster." Twizzledale laughed. "You do not expect us to believe that. The things are ten man-heights above the road, anchored on pedestals which appear to be part of the mountain we ride upon. Surely you don't take such stories seriously."

The older man shrugged, eyebrows high to indicate his own wonder at the idea. "I repeat only what I have read, Gamesman. At certain seasons, these arches glow. All authors agree to that. At certain seasons, those who live hereabouts are in agreement that it is wise to avoid this road. Since that season coincides with the time of storms, during which wise persons avoid travel in any case, perhaps no one has seriously tested the notion that the arches are dangerous then. Or, if not dangerous, something else. Something stranger, perhaps."

Mavin was following along behind, marveling as much as the two riding ahead, but less vocal about it. "Did you know these things were here?" she whispered to Mertyn.

"I read about them," he answered. "But the book didn't say much. Just that no one knows who built them or why. I can't even figure out how anyone could have put them here."

Mavin agreed. The arches might have been made of green stone, or metal, though they seemed more crystal-line than metallic, giving an impression of translucence without actually letting any light through. Two man-heights broad at the base, they narrowed as they rose, dwindling to a knife's edge straight above the road. Where the shadow of the arches lay upon the way, the horses hopped and skipped like zeller kids, sidling across the shadow as though it formed some mazy barrier which only they could see and only such frolicking progress could penetrate. Each transit of the shadow made Mavin think she heard twanging chords of music, rapidly blending, echoing briefly on her skin when they had come through, and—most interesting she thought— each passage of shadow seemed to take time totally out of keeping with the actual width of the shadow on the road.

"Remarkable," breathed Windlow, trying to stay on his jigging horse. "I hear music. Quite remarkable."

"Shadowpeople," breathed Mertyn to Mavin. "Shadowpeople are supposed to have all kinds of musical magic, Mavin. Could the shadowpeople have built these?"

"Shadowpeople aren't builders, are they? I thought they just sang in the wilderness and made music and ate a few travelers now and then."

"I don't think so. I don't think they eat travelers, I mean. They trick people. Lead them over cliffs, or into bogs, but only if the people are doing something bad to them."

"Children's tales, brother boy."

"Maybe. There's some truth in children's tales, though, or they wouldn't go on being told. You're right, though. No children's tale I ever heard mentioned the shadowpeople building anything. Just the same, whenever the horse dances through one of those shadows, I think of shadowpeople."

"Wise beyond your years, young one," said Windlow, coming up from behind where he had stopped yet again to inspect one of the Monuments. "I, too, think of shadowpeople. As a Seer, I have learned thinking of some oddity is often prelude to other oddity following. It is tempting to wonder what actually does happen here in the season of storms."

"I'd like to know where the road goes," said Mavin.

"Why, it goes to Pfarb Durim."

"No, I mean the other end."

"To Betand?"

"Betand is just a human city. If the Monuments were built on a road, then it must have been important where the road went. It couldn't have gone to a human city, because the human city wasn't there. So it must have gone somewhere else." She fell silent, noting that Windlow had fixed her with a somehow calculating eye, as though she had surprised him. Before he could reply, however, a cry came from before them.

"Pfarb Durim!" A cloud of dust bustled toward them, full of hoof clatter. It was Boldery. "Pfarb Durim is just down the hill."

They jigged through the last of the arches to see the city spread before them, its high walls bulking hugely in the center of a saucerlike depression resulting from some long ago subsidence of the cliff's edge. Around the rim of this saucer the road ran, making a wide circle to the east before turning north once more. To their left they could see a narrow road winding up from the valley, from Poffle, and from the circling road several broad avenues ran downward to the city which gulped them in through strangely shaped gates. These gates and the many doors made tall keyholes of black against the lighter stone. Vast iron braziers stood on the wall at each corner, twisted iron baskets hung before the gates, all stuffed full of grease-soaked wood which would be lit at nightfall to send a smoky pillar hovering over the place. The smell of burned fat reached them first, then the smell of the markets outside the gates, spices and fish, raw hides and incense, the stench of commerce carrying a wild babble of voices which rose and fell as the sound of moving water.

"Pfarb Durim," said Windlow. "City of legends. Here, so it is said, when our forefathers came to this place a thousand years ago, they found the city already built by other than we, by not-men, perhaps by those who built the arches.''

"It smells very human to me," said Mertyn, wrinkling his nose.

"It has been occupied by humans for some time," he replied.

They led their animals through the market, fascinated to see so many things being bought and sold, hearing the cries of the merchants as they would have heard strange birds in a forest, with as little understanding. The gate was guarded by several red-nosed men who looked them over casually, inquired whence they had come, and seemed inclined to accept Mavin and Mertyn as part of Windlow's group without any special inquisition as to their origins. Once inside the walls, Mavin handed the reins of her horse to Twizzledale, who was riding a bit behind the others, and bowed to him from the street.

"We appreciate your kindness, Gamesman. Now we must leave you with our thanks."

"Where are you meeting your . . . whoever?" he asked, looking more closely at her than she found comfortable. "You're welcome to stay with us until you are met." Giving the lie to this, Prince Valdon shouted from the street corner.

"Leave the pawnstuff, Wizard! There's wine waiting!"

Twizzledale flushed, but did not move. Mavin said, "Thank you again, Gamesman. But we will not inflict ourselves upon you further. I must obey the instructions I was given." She smiled, more warmly than she had intended, backed away from him, and set out around the corner, Mertyn's hand clutched firmly in her own. There she took refuge in a deep doorway while she tried to decide where to go next.

"Brother child, we need some cheap lodging to roost

in while we find the best road to the Shadowmarches and Battlefox.''

"If you don't want to run into the Seer and his students, we'd better see where they go," said Mertyn, leaning around the corner, his voice betraying the sadness he felt. He had been looking forward to a few more hours with Boldery in pursuit of some form of exciting mischief. "It would have been nice to . . . ''

"Yes, it would have been nice to. But I didn't dare. That Twizzledale kept looking at me as though he could see through to my smalls. I don't think I made a convincing man. There's something more to it than shape, and he was suspicious of something the whole time. I could smell it.''

"But he liked you.''

"That might have been the trouble," she answered. "If he'd despised me, as Prince Valdon does, he would not have looked at me so closely.''

The boy was peering around the corner still, then turned to her, sighing. "They've gone into a big inn right at the wall. I guess we should go on into the city. Should we ask someone?''

"We should," she agreed, and set about doing so. Within a few moments she had the names of three cheap lodging houses, all within a short distance of one another, as well as three sets of instructions how to reach them. They set off in a hopeful frame of mind which changed to a kind of dismay as they left the open ways near the gate and began to wend down damp alleys, shadowed by protruding stories in the buildings to either side and threatened by a constant shower of debris from the windows and roofs. "Gamelords, what a warren," she said. "I had no idea.''

As they made a last turn, Mertyn ran full into a staggering man who gurgled ominously, supporting himself against the wall. Mertyn reached out to catch him, then drew back, fastidiously wiping his face where the man had drooled on him. "Play . . . play . . . " the man gasped, his eyes protruding with the effort. "Play . . . ch'owt . . . " And then he crumpled onto the stones, fingers scrabbling weakly at the slimy cobbles.

"Come on!" ordered Mavin. "We can't help him, but we can send help." And they ran on, coming into a wider area in which the lodging houses they had sought all stood, one bearing a sign THE BALD BADGER near at hand.

The door jangled as they opened it, and a voice screamed at them from some other room. "Wait! Don't move, now, just wait and I'll get to ya. A minute. That's all. I swear, only a minute, and I'll get to ya. Are you there?"

"We're here," Mavin replied in a doubtful voice.

"A minute. I'll get to ya. Everybody's so impatient. Run, run. I'll get to ya." There was no sign of the person getting to them immediately. They looked at one another, then turned as a soft footfall whispered on the stairs behind them.

"Sirs," said a gray voice. "You desire lodging?"

"Just a minute," screamed the other voice. "Run, run."

"A thrilpat," explained the colorless woman who owned the gray voice. "Over trained. A vocabulary of over twenty phrases, none of which are in the least useful. I'd sell it, except it has the mange."

"Are you there?" screamed the voice hysterically. "Everyone is so impatient."

"We need a room," said Mertyn. "And there's a man down the alley who fell down. I think he's sick."

The gray woman smoothed her tightly knotted hair, slick upon her skull as paint. "A room I can provide. Assistance for men who fall ill in alleys is outside my competence, young sir. When I have shown you what we have—little enough, but cheap. Lords, yes, cheap is the name of the house—when I have shown you, I'll get the kitchen girl to run tell the watch about the sick man. Will that satisfy your sense of the appropriate? The honorable? The kindly? This way. Watch the step, second from the top. It wants nailing down."

They followed through half darkness until a door opened, flooding the corridor with light. "Step in. You'll need to share the bed, there's only one, but it's fresh straw and linens washed only last week." The slant-roofed room peaked over the open window which let in the turmoil of the street. The bed was low, wide, and the place smelled clean. "How much?" asked Mavin, in her bargaining voice.

"Coin or trade? Three minimunt in coin. If you were a Healer, I'd give it to you for a bit of work. You're not, though, nor anything else useful to me at the moment. Well, then, three minimunt. With a bit of supper thrown in. Nothing fancy, a cup of this and that and some beer. By the by, my name is Pantiquod Palmfast. They call me Panty. Nothing to do with intimate trousering, young sir, so do not giggle in that unfortunate way. No, it has to do with breath, with breathing, with climbing these ghastly flights of stairs. Well, enough. Three minimunt, is it?" She smiled, a smile as gray as her voice, and went away, closing the door behind her. Mertyn was already on the bed.

"Will you remind her about the sick man, Mavin. I think she'll probably forget it."

"I think you'd better not worry about it, brother child. I've a feeling there are more unfortunates in Pfarb Durim than you could possible give worrying time to. Still, I'll remind her, for what good it may do. Next thing is to see where we might get some maps, don't you think?"

"Shadowpeople, too," he said drowsily, burrowing

into the bed. "I'll pull the latchstring in behind you and take a nap."

"It isn't like you to sleep in the bright day, child."

"Well, Boldery was telling stories last night, about ghost pieces. Boldery tells good stories, but I didn't get much sleep."

"All right then," she agreed. "But I'll hammer on the door when I come back, so be ready. And you're not to go out by yourself, even if I'm late." She did not leave the door until she saw the end of the latchstring slide through the hole, then she went down the way they had come, stopping for a moment to speak to the gray woman who emerged, like a phantom out of smoke, at the bottom of the stairs.

"Yes, I've sent the girl to tell the watch, young sir. Not that it will do much good. They'll send a wagon after him, sooner or later, and it will take him to the infirmary of the Healers—though with all the Healers gone, who knows what good that will do."

"Healers gone? Why?"

She put on a mysterious face. "There is talk in the marketplace of a dispute between the Healers and a certain inhabitant of . . . Poffle. You know of Poffle?"

"I've heard of it," she admitted.

"Ah. Well, Healers were summoned there from Pfarb Durim. Evidently they did not go or would not heal, it is uncertain which. Then others were sought and brought—some say involuntarily, which is a mistake in dealing with Healers—and something unfortunate happened, so it is alleged, which caused all the Healers to leave Pfarb Durim and set a ban on the city."

"But if the dispute is with Poffle, why set a ban on this city?"

"The connection is always assumed, young sir. The place below is somewise dependent upon Pfarb Durim. Or, other end up, possibly. Whatever. May I offer you any help or direction?'' she added, looking curiously at Mavin's cloak. And, upon Mavin's telling her that she needed a mapmaker or guide or geographer or any combination of them, the lodging keeper gave her directions to Chart Street.

It was almost dusk when she returned, the lights of the city were being lit and the great firebaskets upon the walls had been set ablaze. In the red, smoky glare, ordinary citizens began to assume the guise of devils. Every face seemed either frightened or menacing or closed around some ominous secret. Laughing at herself for these fantasies, Mavin nonetheless hurried to return to the lodging house, thinking of Mertyn and dinner with about equal intensity. She had purchased half a dozen cheap maps of the Shadowmarches, from different chartmakers, on the theory that the features common to all might be assumed—only might be assumed— to indicate a close approximation to reality. On the other hand, she told herself, it might not be wise to discount the odd, dangerous feature shown on only one. That one might have been the result of an exploration while the others were only popular fiction or speculation.

She knocked at the door of their room for a long time before Mertyn dragged it open. He stood peering at her blearily, eyes and face swollen and red. She touched his forehead and cheeks and felt a feverish heat. He seemed unable to focus on her.

''Brother child, what's the matter with you?''

''I feel—all sort of sick,'' he said. ''Everything keeps fading.''

''Have you been asleep since I left?''

''I slept a long time,'' he said, staggering back toward the bed. ''Then I woke up feeling funny, and it comes and goes.''

''Stay here,'' she instructed him, though he showed

no inclination to go anywhere. "I'll get you some broth from the kitchen and see where the nearest Healers are to be found."

"Danderbats don't seek Healing. . . ." he murmured.

"Battlefoxes do," she said grimly, remembering her conversation with her thalan. As she went down the stairs, however, she remembered a more recent conversation, the one with Pantiquod. The woman came out of her hidey hole as though summoned.

"You'll be wanting supper, young sirs," she began.

"I'll be wanting some broth for Mertyn," Mavin cut her off. "He's sick. Did you tell me true, earlier, when you said there were no Healers in Pfarb Durim?"

"According to the tittle-tattle of the marketplace, there is not one Healer left in Pfarb Durim. Healers are clanny, young sir, and if one of them was injured in Poffle, why—I suppose none would come near us after that. 'Who injures a Healer goes without Healing.' Isn't that the old saw? Well, perhaps not. Maybe it's only something I thought I had heard somewhere."

"But the end of all this is what you said earlier. No Healers in Pfarb Durim. Where would the closest ones be, then?"

The gray-faced woman nodded in mixed sympathy and satisfaction. "He's truly ill, then. I thought that might be coming. We seem to have ghoul-plague in the city. So rumor hath."

"Ghoul-plague? I have never heard of it."

"I thought of it when the boy spoke of the sick man in the alley. I was almost certain of it when the wagon came suspiciously soon. Plague has been muttered of for days. They say it began in Poffle. The Healers were summoned and would not—some say could not—heal. An attempt was made to force them. Now the plague has come to Pfarb Durim, and the Healers are gone." Then, seeing the horror on Mavin's face, she relented.

"Let us not be so quick. Come, I'll get you some broth. Perhaps he is only weary from his journey."

But when they returned to the room, Mavin could not get Mertyn's attention at all. He was in some deep well of delirium from which she could not arouse him.

"It's too quick," complained Mavin. "We only arrived today."

"The disease is sudden in those it takes," said Pantiquod from where she hovered in the doorway, not coming any closer than she needed to see the boy's face. "And he said he touched the man in the alley."

"Do they recover?" Mavin whispered. "Does it kill many?"

"Some recover," Pantiquod said. "Most die. It is said that the shadowpeople can cure it, which is like saying a flask of sun will gild thrilps. First one has to fill one's flask." The woman left her, turning in the doorway to say, "Do not try to move him. Sometimes, so I have heard, persons ill with ghoul-plague are transported, perhaps in search of a Healer, or some more salubrious air. If they are moved, they invariably die. So I am told. Do not move him. In any case, you could not. The gates will soon be locked against any leaving." And the door swung shut behind her, leaving an impression upon its surface as though she stood there still, dim and smokelike, inhabiting the lodging house like mist, a smile almost of satisfaction upon her face.

It did no good to feed Mertyn the broth. It ran out of his mouth. She could not get him to swallow. She sat with him cradled against her, terrified and helpless, not knowing what to do next. When she began to pull herself together, it was fully dark outside.

She did not know whether to believe the woman or not, but for the time being she would not attempt to move Mertyn. He was hot, unconscious, but he breathed steadily and when she put her ear to his chest, his heart thudded away evenly. So. She covered him warmly, set herself frantically to make some sensible plan.

First she must determine whether what the woman said was true. She left the room, wedging the door shut behind her. At the foot of the stairs, she looked inside Pantiquod's hidey hole. It was empty, more then merely empty. It had an air of vacancy about it. Suddenly suspicious, she found her way to the rear of the place. The kitchen was empty also, and the little area way opening from it. She went back up the stairs, opening each room she came to. Empty. So. If there had been plague rumored for the past days, then those who heard the rumor would have left the city. The woman herself? Had she stayed? Or did she have some secret way out?

No matter where she might be, Mertyn and Mavin were alone in the place now, and the street outside was quieter than it had been since she had entered the city. She opened the heavy door onto the street. It creaked, and the wall torch showed her the crudely painted words, ''Plague here,'' on its rough outer surface. The warning had been painted after she had returned, within moments, perhaps of that time. Mavin found some curse phrases she had not remembered knowing and used them freely, harshly, whispering into the silent street. She would have to leave Mertyn alone in the place while she sought some kind of help. Perhaps the sign on the door would protect him as well as anything could. She closed the door softly behind her and went back down the dark alley, the way they had originally come, unaware until she was halfway to the city wall that she was going to find the Seer Windlow. Then she realized that it was the only sensible thing to do.

She found the inn at the city wall without trouble, could not have avoided finding it, for there was a great mob gathered around it full of threats and brandished weapons, like a gathering of devils in the light of the great braziers and the torches. Above them the city walls were crowded with people looking outward, shouting down to those below. "It's King Frogmott from the north. He has Armigers and Elators with him." And these cries were contradicted by others, "No, they come from the Graywater Demesne of the Sorcerer Lanuzh!" Mavin forced her way through the crowd, tucking in a rib here and bending a shoulder there. Everyone was so full of panic that they paid her no attention. From the wall she looked out to see the City gates guarded from some distance by an array of warriors and Gamesmen, torches flickering along their lines, lighting the pennants flickering over their heads.

"Why are they here?" she asked the nearest watcher. "Who are they?"

"I've heard six people say six different things about who they are," her informant muttered. "As to why, well, young man, that should be obvious to anyone. We've plague in the city, and those out there are determined we shall not bring it out of these walls."

"Surely there are Elators within the walls who could transport themselves away in an instant? Armigers who could fly over their lines? Others, perhaps, who escape such sieges as this every day of their lives? The place cannot be closed tight!" Mavin was beginning to feel the crowd's panic as her own. Her heart pounded and her muscles twitched with the need to do something.

"Well, and if it gets bad enough, they'll probably try. The Healers have set a proscription on all who leave the city, however, and not many will risk that until they must. Even an Elator must come out somewhere, and it is said they have the countryside for leagues around under watch."

"It's true, then? What someone told me. A Healer was injured—forced, down in Poffle."

"So the story goes. There is plague there, in Poffle. And now there is plague here."

"Has anyone approached the Healers? Surely they know there are people here innocent of any involvement with Poffle. Travelers."

"Young man, ask someone who knows. I am a merchant, here doing trade, and as innocent of involvement as yourself. Wait! See there. A Herald comes. Now you will have some answer, and so will I."

A knot of glaring light had separated from the flaming line along the hill and was coming toward them, lighting the upper half of a Herald's body so that he seemed a half person, floating upon the dark. The light came from a large, shallow brazier floating between two Tragamors, and its evident purpose was to light the Herald's face so that he could be recognized. He stopped outside the walls, far enough away that all could see, yet close enough to be heard. Mavin had been told of Heralds' Talent, but she had never heard the trumpet voice with which Gamesmen of this persuasion made their pronouncements. When the voice came, it startled her as well as others along the wall so that they moved as one with a reflexive grunt.

"People of Pfarb Durim give ear," the Herald cried. "I am the Herald Dumarch-don, servant of the great King, Frogmott of the Marshes, and of his allies in this endeavor, the Sorcerer Lanuzh, the mighty Armiger, Galesbreath of Rockwind Demesne, and other Gamelords and men of unquestioned honor and unlimited might. I cry siege upon the city of Pfarb Durim and upon that pit of Hell which lies at its feet. Siege shall be maintained until all within have died or until a cure has come. Let none within seek to escape, for our vengeance will be dreadful upon him and upon his house, his Demesne, and his kindred." The Herald wore a tabard of jewels. His face was proud and high-nosed, and his voice like an orchestra of brass, mellow and challenging at once. Mavin could not get her fill of looking at him, so marvelous he was, but he turned his back on all within the city and rode away, back to that flickering line of light along the mountain.

When she turned back to ask yet another question, the man had gone, and she stood for long moments upon the wall staring out at the gathered host. Even as she watched, a hilltop was crowned with moving figures, newly arrived besiegers tightening the grip upon the city. She fought her way down the stairs and through the crowd gathered around the inn. Huge, burly men guarded the door, pretending not to hear her as she asked for the Seer Windlow. Giving up in frustration, she slipped away, around the side of the place and into a narrow, blank alleyway where the trash from the place was dumped. There was a small window, high above. She looked around to see that she was not observed, then lengthened an arm and used it to pull herself up and through the narrow opening. She came down into the place, casually, stopping a scurrying servant in the hall.

"I am seeking the Seer Windlow. I carry an important message for him. Can you tell me where he is?"

"There's no Seer here, young sir. Was you wanting that one with the young men and the boy? He was here eating a meal, but then he went with the others. To the Mudgery Mont, so they said at dinner. And sensible it was of them, too, for the Mont is above all this clamor." And she was off down the hallway, answering a screamed summons from below.

Mavin used the same window to leave the place and set about finding the Mudgery Mont, growing more frantic by the moment as she thought of Mertyn left alone.

Now it was necessary to fight her way through the

streets, packed from wall to wall with the inhabitants of the inner city as they tried to get to the walls, to the gates, to learn for themselves that the city had been closed like a trap with themselves inside. She gave it up before she had gone two streets, melting into a dark sideway and from that swarming up the side of a building and onto the roofs. When she had come to a less crowded place, she descended, picking out a small group who seemed disinclined to join the general pack.

"The Mudgery Mont? Surely. At the top of the hill which caps the cliffs, young man. They'll never let you in there, though. It's guarded like a treasury."

Mavin nodded her thanks and was off again, swarming onto the roofs once more to lope across them in some long legged form more usual in forests than in such a place as this. She could see the hill against the western sky, crowned with squat towers and another set of walls. It was closer, actually, to the place she had left Mertyn than the gateway inn had been, and she wasted some small breath giving thanks for this as she ran and climbed and swung across gaping chasms of street.

Behind her came the hooting of a great horn, an outcry of bells, a welling shout as from a thousand throats. Something had happened where the mob was gathered, but she did not look back. Soon she was at the foot of the hill where streets widened to sweep upward around mansions and palaces and one brightly lit and elegant hotel. Before it stood a dozen Gamesmen in livery, Heralds and Tragamors, leaping to do the bidding of those who went in and out. Mavin came to ground and walked into the light, approaching the door as though she had business there. They did not let her go by unchallenged.

"Just hold a minute there, young man," said one of the Tragamors, moving toward her purposefully. "What business have you here?"

"I have come to Mudgery Mont to find the Seer Windlow. I have . . . a message for him."

"Does he expect you?"

"I think—yes, he may well. Can you tell me if he is here?"

"Give me your name. Wait here. It may be he will receive you, and it may be he will not."

"Tell him, please, that Mavin waits without. With news which he should have."

She waited. The Tragamor showed no indication of passing on her message or of going himself. Time passed. She fidgeted from foot to foot, strode back and forth. Then she saw another petitioner approach the Tragamor, give him money, and the man went within on the moment.

"Gamelords," she said to herself. "I have no coin to pay the man. What I have must be kept for Mertyn's sake." She melted back into the darkness, into the shadows of the streets and up to the roofs once more. Trees grew in the gardens of the Mont, and she was able to go across to the roof of the hotel itself, leaping like some great thrilpat among the branches. From there it was only a few moments to find a stairway leading down, and from there only a matter of time until she encountered a servant.

"I seem to have lost my way," she said, trying to give an appearance of puzzled calm. "I am looking for the Seer Windlow, or any of his party."

"Certainly, young sir," she replied. "Will you follow me." She trotted away, down a flight of stairs, to knock on a door and beckon Mavin forward. The door opened and she said, "This young man wandering about the hotel, sir, looking for a guest." Before she could react, Mavin found herself held fast by yet another Tragamor in the livery of the place confronting an irritable-looking Armiger who held a glass of wine in one hand and a sword in the other.

"A spy," he grated. "The hotel is full of them. They gather in closets and leap out at one from under the stairs. And who are you working for, young spy?"

She had no time to invent anything new. Taken by surprise, she fell back upon the story she knew. "I am the servant of the Wizard Himaggery, sir. I traveled here in company with the Seer Windlow and his group of students. I seek him now, with a message." She tried to keep the face which she wore calm, slightly aloof, not dismayed, even though her nerves screamed at the thought of Mertyn, alone in the empty lodging house, burning with fever.

"Humph," the Armiger snorted. "A silly tale, but silly enough to be true. How did you get in?"

"The guards were busy talking with someone, sir. I just came in." She tried to sound surprised at this. Evidently the propensity of the guards for unguardly behavior was sufficiently well understood that they believed her. "Raif, go up and get someone from the Seer's party to come down here and vouch for this youngster.

"You'd better be telling the absolute truth, young man, for if you are not we'll have a Demon delving into your skull within the hour, and he'll not rest till he knows who spies upon the guests of Mudgery Mont." He went grumpily to his chair, taking the wine with him, but sheathing the sword. Mavin breathed a bit more freely, and the two men who held her relaxed somewhat. It was not long before the door opened, and the Tragamor called Raif returned with a youth, scarcely more than a boy, whom Mavin had not seen before.

"Gamesman Huld offered to take a look at him," said Raif, standing aside. Behind him the youth paused, posed in the doorway, and fingered the jeweled dagger hung at his golden belt. He was elegantly, almost foppishly dressed, wearing a Demon's half helm so over ornamented that it appeared top heavy. Beneath it a narrow, white face looked out through swollen-lidded eyes, a lizard's look, calculating, without warmth.

"Who does he say he is?" The voice was as chill as the eyes, as uncaring. "Who does the pawnish churl say he is?"

Mavin took tight rein on her temper, recoiled within herself as if she had seen a serpent rearing before her, and spoke quietly, without emphasis. "I am the servant of the Wizard Himaggery, Gamesman. I seek the Seer Windlow to give him a message."

"You can give it to me," he said carelessly. "The Seer is occupied."

She breathed deeply, aware of danger. "My deepest apologies, Gamesman. I may give the message only to the Seer."

Anger flared in the pale youth's face, turning it into a livid mask. He turned to the Armiger, sneered, "It does not know its place, does it, Armiger? I suggest you teach it its place, and bring it to me when it is ready to give me its so-called *message*. This is no Wizard's servant, for Wizards have better taste. . . ." His hand began to play with his dagger, half drawing it from its sheath, and Mavin knew he was about to Read her to find the truth.

"Do they, now?" The drawling voice came from the doorway, which still stood open. Seeing the tall figure which lounged there brought sudden tears of relief to Mavin's eyes. It was Twizzledale. "Do Wizards indeed have better taste? The youth told you, I suppose, that he is the servant of the Wizard Himaggery. Did he not, Huld?"

"Nonsense," spat the Demon. "Lies and trickery. Likely there is no Wizard Himaggery. . . ."

"Oh, indeed there is, Huld, and I am he." Twizzle-dale strolled into the room, one hand playing with the knife at his own belt, almost in mockery of the Demon.

The pale youth barked laughter. "You? You are the Fon, whatever a Fon may be, of some place no one has ever heard of."

"Am I a Wizard, Huld?" Twizzledale's voice purred, all the mockery gone from it, menace dripping from every sound.

"So you say!"

"Would you care to test the notion, Huld?"

The bulky Tragamor crossed the room in one heaving motion. "My lord, Huld. The revered Ghoul Blourbast, your thalan, would not forgive us if some misunderstanding were to result in any injury to you, or even any discomfort. Surely the matter is not worth a major confrontation. The Seer is here under the protection of the High King Prionde. The High King's sons travel with him. This Wizard is with them, also, and it is said that you will join the group. . . ."

"I will not," the Demon sneered. "I have looked it over. I have smelled it. It was my thalan's wish that I be *educated* at some advanced school, but this Seer is no Gamesmaster. He is a charlatan, a fake. I will have nothing to do with it." He turned and stalked from the room, leaving the Armiger still mumbling.

"Raif, go with him. No doubt he'll leave the city by way of the tunnel. Let him go. But double the guard behind him." Baring his teeth, he frowned at the man's back, then turned back to Twizzledale and Mavin. "You say you're this man's master? Well, then get him out of here, and I don't want to find him wandering about the hotel again. You've just put me between the jaws of a cracker, and I like not the feel of it. Do you know who he is?" And he pointed the way Huld had gone.

"I learned," said the Fon. "Tonight. When the Seer learned. We had not been told that the young Demon, Huld, was ward or thalan or what have you of the Archghoul, Blourbast, holder of Hell's Maw."

The Armiger lifted off the ground, hung in the air, burning with annoyance. "Don't say that. Don't say that word."

"Hell's Maw," repeated Twizzledale. "From which no good thing comes. Is that not the saying here in Pfarb Durim? I have heard it seven times since entering the city, Guardmaster. Come now. Settle. You are using power to no purpose. We will leave you in peace."

He took Mavin by the shoulder and led her out of the room. "Mavin, what possessed you to try that here? The place is guarded like an old pombi's one kit."

"I know," she whispered, reaching for his hand. "Listen, Fon. There's plague in Pfarb Durim. . . ." And as they walked she murmured rapidly of all that had brought her to Mudgery Mont.

When they came to the door of the suite of chambers which were occupied by the Seer and his students, Twizzledale opened the door softly, peering around it before entering. He drew her into a side room, shut the door behind them, and then went to still another door, half hidden behind a hanging. "I didn't want Valdon to see you," he explained. "It was he who sent Huld down to identify you. There was much sympathetic feeling between the two." He passed through the door, leaving it ajar, and she heard a rapid murmur of voices, Windlow saying "No! Here!" and more rustling of clothing as the voices went on. The Seer came into the room, belting a robe around him.

"Where is the place young Mertyn lies ill?" he demanded.

She went to the window, oriented herself by the slope of the hill and the line of distant towers, pointed.

"There. Near the round-roofed building. Perhaps six or seven streets over. The woman who runs the place—who ran the place. She left—said not to move him."

"I doubt it would hurt him to be wrapped well and carried here, if it were done quickly. Twizzledale will go, and I'll send men from the Mont."

"Valdon won't like it," said the Fon. "He grows more annoyed with every passing hour."

"Valdon is frustrated that the world has not yet fallen at his feet," said Windlow. "His expectations of this journey were unrealistic. He awaited some great event, some recognition of himself. He must blame someone. Well, we will not speak of it to him."

"What will they think?" Mavin murmured. "About your going out to get a boy, just a boy."

"Why, Mavin." Windlow was surprised. "What would they think if the Wizard Himaggery did not go out to rescue his thalan? Since the Fon has said he is the Wizard Himaggery—and who am I to say he is not, particularly if both you and he say he is—and since everyone, including Boldery, knows that Mertyn is the Wizard Himaggery's thalan, why then of course he must be rescued." He turned to Twizzledale, frowning. "Though how you will explain it all to Valdon, I do not know. I leave it to your necessarily fertile imagination."

And from that moment it was only a short time before they came to the empty lodging house with a troop of the Mont's guards and carried Mertyn back to that place, up the back way, quietly, into a room separated from the body of the hotel, where the Seer awaited them. Only Twizzledale had touched him, though the Seer now laid a hand upon his forehead and sighed.

"The woman said ghoul-plague, did she? And that is what the host outside the gate is besieging us for? Then I am deeply worried, lad."

"What is this disease?" Mavin asked. "I had never heard of it."

"It begins, some say, with the eating of human flesh. For this reason it is called ghoul-plague. In my reading of history, however, I have found that it may not be human flesh but the flesh of shadowpeople which causes the disease. Once begun, it is like other plagues, crossing from those who have eaten the forbidden flesh to those who have not. It is carried from place to place, and none know how."

"Mertyn touched the sick man, in the alley. The man drooled on him. On his face."

"That may have been enough. A very ancient book spoke of disease being spread by the bites of small creatures, little blood suckers or flitter bats. I have seen plagues of similar kind. Some do recover." He did not sound hopeful.

"The woman said the shadowpeople are said to cure this plague," said Mavin. For the past hour she had been making plans, moving pieces of information about in her head. "I'm going to go find them, Gamesmaster."

"Find the shadowpeople?" The Fon was amazed. "They can't be found by anyone wishing to do so."

"Perhaps not. But I must try. Will you care for Mertyn while I am gone? I would not ask this thing of you, except that you are kindly and good, and you cannot leave the city anyhow."

"And you," murmured Windlow. "How will you leave the city?"

"The way that Demon did," she said. "The Armiger said he went through tunnels."

"By all the Gamegods, child. Those tunnels lead to Hell's Maw. And I do not know, nor do any in this city know for all I can tell, whether there is any way out of Hell's Maw at all."

Chapter 6

Though both of them tried to dissuade her, speaking quietly so as not to disturb Mertyn, she would not be moved.

"I must go. Never mind about Poffle. I'll get through Poffle. Never mind about shadowpeople, I'll . . . " And still they argued.

Until suddenly old Windlow stiffened where he stood, his face turning rigid and pale, his hands stretching out as though to touch something the others could not see.

"He's having a vision," whispered the Fon. "Quiet. It affects him in this way sometimes when he is very upset." They watched, not touching him, as he swayed upon his feet, his eyes darting from side to side as though watching some wild movement or affray they could not see. Then his eyes shut, he swayed, caught at the bed to keep himself from falling, and gasped deeply, like a man coming from under water and desperate for air.

"We must let her go, Twizzledale," he said at last.

"Let . . . *her* go? Mavin? Oh, come now, Windlow.

Or have I been unwizardly?'' He turned to give Mavin a keen look, swiftly up and down.

Mavin, staring at the Seer, knew that the Fon had penetrated at least part of her identity, but let the feminine identification go by without protest. "You saw something. What was it?''

"I'm not sure," he sighed. "It was dark and there was a great deal of confusion. But Mertyn was there, and his sister, Mavin. And Mavin had a trick or two in her left ear, or so Mertyn said. There was something evil. Valdon was involved. Something terrible, huge. Lords, Twizzledale, but at times I hate being a Seer." He grabbed at his head with both hands as though he would tear it off. "Sometimes I think I am not a Seer at all, but something else."

The Fon accused her, quoting Windlow. "His *sister* Mavin, eh? What are you, young person? Charlatan, as Huld accused us of being? Or something else?''

"Hush," said Windlow distractedly. "Don't snarl at her, Wizard. Whatever she has done, she's done for the boy. Go with her. Help her if you can. But don't snarl. Don't worry about Mertyn more than you can help, Mavin. Whatever can be done for the boy, I'll do."

"You won't move him, Seer?''

"No farther than he's been moved, child. Go with Twizzledale. Take what you need from our goods, food, whatever. There's a puzzle about you that my Seeing didn't do a thing to solve, you know. Until we meet in happier times, then." He embraced her. She felt a dew of clammy perspiration on his cheeks, a trembling in his hands, but his mouth was firm as he turned her out the door, Twizzledale following, still in his mood of irritation.

"I don't like it when people don't tell me things," he grumbled. "Particularly important things."

She sighed, moved by his exasperation, not to an

answering anger but to some soothing words, some kindliness. He looked so spiky, hands rooting at his hair, eyes sparking with annoyance.

"Wizard. I know you are angry with me, but how could I trust you? Someone just met on the road? I barely felt I could trust the Seer, and I wouldn't have come to him if I had had any choice. Please." She stopped, holding him by his arm. "Where are we going?"

"Back to our rooms. To pack you some—whatever you need. Food, I suppose. A change of clothing."

"I won't need any of that. Wizard, if you want to help me, come with me to the entrance, the tunnels, the way to go through that place . . . Poffle. Don't go on being angry. It has nothing to do with you, truly."

They stood in confrontation, he clenching and unclenching his fists, shifting his weight as though he wanted to hit her; she, head cocked, poised, prepared for flight if he decided to grab her. So they stared, glared, until he began to smile, then to laugh. "I'd like to strangle you." He coughed. "You're impossible."

She smiled warily. "I'm really doing the only thing I can."

"You're shifter, aren't you? I should have guessed. The minute Windlow said 'sister,' I should have guessed. I did guess. Except that . . ."

"Except that you don't like shifters," she said in a flat, emotionless tone. "Other Gamesmen, yes. But not shifters."

"Hold! I've never known a shifter. Surely, shifters are supposed to be—well, what are they supposed to be. Stranger than the rest of us? Less understandable?"

"Less trustworthy?" Her smile was sweet, poisonous. "Less reliable? Less honorable?"

"More tricky," he said, amused again. "More devious, more challenging, more entertaining."

"Less destructible," she said in a firm voice, putting an end to the catalogue. "Which is why I think I can get through Poffle to the outside world. Which is why I think maybe I can find shadowpeople, though others possibly have been unable to do so."

"How old are you?" he asked, apropos of nothing.

"Fifteen," she said, before she thought.

"Young. Have you had talent long? I mean . . ."

"You mean, have I had it long enough to learn to use it. Yes, Wizard, I have. Probably better than you have learned to use your own. I had to." And she turned away from him to march out into the dark through a side door, he following mutely, feeling it a better idea to hide his curiosity than to annoy her with any more questions. Once outside he led her in a circuitous route through the grounds of the Mont and onto a narrow walkway curving along the rim of the escarpment. The way was unfrequented, littered with small trash, ending in a parapet surrounded by a low wall.

"Down there." He pointed.

She looked over to see the narrow crevasse which fell below the wall, a walkway there lined with needled, misshapen trees. At the end of the walkway a lonely lantern burned beside a grilled arch, and outside the grill a platoon of guardsmen moved restlessly back and forth. The archway led into darkness.

"This is the Ghoul Blourbast's private highway into Pfarb Durim," said the Fon. "It was pointed out to us by Huld. The Seer was not happy to learn of that young man's true identity."

"How was it that you did not know?"

"The arrangements were made through third parties, Negotiators and Ambassadors. That alone should have warned Windlow that something was amiss. What use has an honest Gamesman for Ambassadors!"

"It seems Huld didn't care much for the arrangement either."

"Valdon is an example of humility compared to Huld. After some time in Valdon's company I thought him the epitome of arrogance, but I was wrong. I believe Huld has never asked for anything, no matter how outrageous, which he has not been given. Who is he, really? No one seems to know, except that Blourbast holds him dear. And he went back down that hell hole, Mavin, so watch out for him."

"He will not see me," she said soberly, then, taking him by the arm, "Fon, can you help me? With the shadowpeople? What language do they speak? What would they ask of me in return for healing Mertyn?"

He shook his head. "I wish I knew, Mavin. I would help you in any way I could, if only because you tricked me and teased me and made my mind work in odd ways. You must find them first and then try to do them a service, as you would for anyone, Gamesman or pawn. If they are peoplelike—and I have heard that they are in some ways—then they will seek to do you a service in repayment. How you will speak with them, I do not know. I have never seen one of them. At times I have doubted they exist." He pulled her to him and squeezed her, quickly releasing her, so that she felt only breathless and wondering at the suddenness of it. "Let us make a pact, however. If you have need of me, you will send word—let me think! The word shall be the name of that place you stayed, BALD BADGER. Or, if there is no way to send word, then the first letter of your name in fire or smoke or stone or whatever. Given that word, that signal, I'll get to you somehow."

"You can't get out," she said. "The city is closed."

"You can't get out either," he replied. "And yet you are going. So. Strange are the Talents of Wizards. Leave the way of it to me.'' And he released her, standing away from her, and looking at her in a way no one had looked at her before. Mavin shook her head, trying to clear it, then gave it up and turned from him to slide over the low parapet at the edge of the declivity. She cast one look over her shoulder to see him walking steadily away. She had not wanted him to watch her as she changed. Seemingly he had understood that.

She shifted into something which could climb walls, rather spiderlike if she had thought about it, which she had no time to do. At the bottom of the ditch, she skulked along behind the twisted trees until the light of the torches splashed amber on the stones before her. She had already decided what to do next. Using an arm much stronger than her own, she heaved a paving stone high onto the opposite bank, some distance behind her. It crashed through the branches with a satisfactory sound of someone thrashing about. The guards ran toward it, not looking behind them, and she slipped through the bars of the gate into darkness, resuming her own shape once hidden in shadow. Only a shifter could have come through the gate—a shifter or a serpent. The bars had been set close together.

There was no light in the tunnel. Far ahead she thought she could see a faint grayness in the black. She fumbled her way forward, stopping close to the walk-way, feeling a slimy dampness on her hands where they touched the walls or floor. Furred feet made no sound. Soon she was walking four-footed, making a nose which would smell out trails and paths. A sharp sound broke the silence, echoed briefly like a shout into a well, and was gone. Still, it had given her direction in the darkness. The grayness grew more light. She turned toward it, out of the widened corridor and into a side way. It was torchlight, reflected off wet walls around several sinuous turns. The torch burned outside another barred gate which was no more trouble than the first had been. Now the corridor was lighted, badly, with smoky torches at infrequent intervals.

She became aware of sound, a far, indefinite clanging, an echoing clamor, a whumping sound as though something heavy fell repeatedly into something soft. Through it all came a thin cry of song, high, birdlike, quickly silenced. She shivered, not knowing why. The sounds were not ugly or threatening, and yet heard together they made her want to weep. She sneaked along the way, now finding windows cut into the stone which looked out into black pits. As she went, she tossed bits of gravel through the openings, listening for the sound. Her ears told her some were merely small rooms or closets while others were bottomless. The sounds came closer, and suddenly—

"Wait a minute, will ya. I'll be with you. Run, run, so impatient. Wait a minute!" The voice screeched, whined, almost at her shoulder, and Mavin fell against the wall, crouched, ready to be attacked.

"I'll be right with ya," the voice screamed.

She reached out, patting the air around her. Another of the openings was just above her head, and hung inside it, far enough inside that no light struck it at all, was a cage. Mavin found the ring on which it was hung, drew it down and into the light. Inside it crouched a ragged-looking beasty, eyes dilated into great, brown orbs, teeth bared, patches of its hide missing as though they had been burned away. "Run," it screamed at her. "Run, run."

Without thinking, Mavin opened the cage and shook the creature out onto the stones where it lay for a moment, too shocked to move. Then in one enormous leap, it crossed the corridor and disappeared down a side way, shrieking as it went. Thoughtfully, Mavin hung the open cage back where she had found it and followed.

"Run, run," it screamed, fleeing at top speed into darkness. "I'll get to ya."

"I hope you do," she muttered. "To one Pantiquod, one strange, gray woman. To one someone who talks, who can be overheard, who knows the way out of here."

She had need of her nose again, for the little animal lost itself in darkness. The stench of it—part illness, part dirty cage, part the beasty itself—lingered on the stones, however, and Mavin tracked the little animal through dark ways into lighter ones to a heavy door upon which the little creature hung, still trying to shriek, though its voice had wearied to a whisper. "Run," it whimpered. "Run. I'll get to ya."

Mavin stood to one side, pressed down upon the latch and let the door swing open. The thrilpat was through it in an instant. Hearing no alarms, Mavin followed. She was now in a well lit corridor ending in a broad flight of stairs. A small balcony protruded to her left, half hidden behind embroidered draperies. She oozed into the cover of these, hearing voices from below.

"I thought I told you to get rid of that animal!" The voice was heavy gasping, full of malice and ill humor. Peering between the railings, Mavin could see where the voice came from—a vast, billowy form lying in a canopied bed. Only the bottom half of the form was visible to her. She could see all of the other persons in the room, however, and was unsurprised to recognize the gray woman from the lodging house, now dressed in an odd, winged cap with a feathered cape at her shoulders. It was Pantiquod, the mangy animal now clinging to her ankle as it sobbed and pled.

"I gave it to one of your servants, brother, and told him to dispose of it."

"Which servant was that?"

"I don't really know. One of those who stand outside this room from time to time."

"Well, find out which one. Have him chained to the long wall in the tunnel. If you can't find out which one, have the whole lot of them chained. Let them hang there till they rot."

"Which they assuredly will. Have you not had enough of rottenness, brother Ghoul? Has it not brought you to this pass? Perhaps it would be well to dwell less on rottenness for a time?"

"Shall a trifle of sickness make me forsake my life's work?" The bulk upon the bed heaved with laughter, and Mavin, watching it, found a kind of fascinated nausea in the sight. The figure heaved itself upright, and the sight of its face made her stomach heave, for it was covered with hideous growths from which a vile ichor oozed. The hands which stroked an amulet at the creature's throat were as badly afflicted. "My bone pits are not yet full, Panty, my sister, my dove. Panty, my dear one, mother of my delicious twins, Huld and Huldra, my dear boy and his delightful sister. And though she has obviously learned aplenty about the world—and will soon enough bear us yet another generation—my dear boy is not yet fully educated. Though it seems he does not want to go into the world to mix with his inferiors."

"It was a foolish idea," she said calmly, seemingly unafraid of this monster on the bed. "You have not reared him to care what others do, or think, or say. How then should he care for education, for is that not the study of what others care about? Hmmm?"

"He says we have taught him enough, you and I. Har, ahrah, enough, he says. Enough that he can use what we have taught him to conquer the world. Harar, aha." The vast figure shivered with obscene laughter, and Mavin trembled upon the balcony.

"I have taught him to dissemble, my lord. To pretend. To play the Gamesman of honor. To mock the manners of others, if it seems wise—or amusing—to do so. What have you taught him?"

"To care for nothing, my love. To be sickened by nothing, repelled by nothing, to be capable of anything at all. Between us, he has been well educated."

"Well then, why this mockery? Why all this effort expended to put him in the company of Prionde's sons? He cared not for them. Should he have?"

"Softly, my dove, my cherub. He did all that was needed. He found in Valdon's mind the way to the King, to Prionde. That was all he needed to do for now. It will be useful for some future Game. They will not suspect him of plotting, not at his age. But he and I—we have planned, sister. We have planned."

"But does it not seem now all those plans are for naught?"

"Araugh," the man screamed in rage. "Beware, sister. Do not be quick to condemn me to death. Blourbast does not die of ghoul-plague. My thalan made me immune to ghoul-plague when I was younger than Huld. I have eaten forbidden meat all my life, and the plague has not touched me!" The bulk heaved, quivered, drew itself upright, then collapsed once more.

"It has not touched you until now," she said, her face as cold and empty of emotion as a mask. "Until now. It amused you to hold the shadowpeople to ransom for their relic. So they came at your command. I told you they were sick, but you sent them to your kitchens nonetheless. You gave the meat to those destined to be sent above, to Pfarb Durim. Well enough. But it was foolish to dine from the same dish, brother. You have not had ghoul-plague before, but you had not used the disease to empty a city before, either. In fact," she turned an ironic glance upon him, "there had been no ghoul-plague for some tens of years. For most of our lifetimes, yours and mine, Blourbast. Now the disease comes again. Perhaps it is a new strain to which you are not immune.''

''Ghoul-plague is ghoul-plague,'' he growled. ''I am immune, I say. I ate only what was necessary so that they should not suspect what meat I fed them. I have eaten this meat many times before.''

''No,'' she contradicted him. ''You have not. I tell you again, brother, this is not any disease which has come upon us before. You are not immune, and now the Healers have spread the ban against you. You should not have tried to force healing out of them.''

''In Hell's Maw, Gamesmen play as I will.''

''But in Hell's Maw they did not. I told you that shadowpeople are reputed to cure this disease. What have you done to learn the truth of this?''

''I have a few dozens in my cellars, madame. Since they speak no tongue I can understand, what good to question them? I had a little man once who spoke their tongue, but he is dead now. My Demons have attempted to Read their little minds, to no end. So let them hang there and starve.''

''You have given up eating them, then? You do not fatten them in their cages?''

''Let them starve, I say. I hold their relic here,'' and he stroked his breast once again, the motion of those horrid hands holding Mavin's eyes fixed. ''Here. So let them starve. Let them all die. It is nothing to me.''

''Nothing? What if you are ill to death, Blourbast?''

''I will recover, woman. I will recover, shadowpeople or no. This is only a temporary inconvenience.''

''But there is Huld, brother. If he sickens, will he recover?''

''You are late with your motherly concern, sister. He is gone to the far reaches of Poffle where the ways open upon the woodlands. I sent him thence, with his lovely sister-wife. He will be served only by his own people. Then, when Pfarb Durim is emptied and the winds have washed it clean, I will give it to him for a gift, as I promised him. He may fill it with his followers, and the revenues will be his and his fortune great, for no city garners more from trade than Pfarb Durim." Exhausted by this speech the bulky form seemed to collapse in upon itself. "Leave me, woman. You were ever contentious."

The woman bowed, moved out of the chamber through a door at the far side, taking one of the torches with her as she went. A kind of gloom fell in the chamber, a heaving dusk, the thick breathing of Blourbast filling it as might the petulant waves of a foul and polluted sea.

Mavin waited for that breathing to soften before creeping down the stairs and into the chamber. She was invisible against the shadows, silent as a shadow herself, as she crept around the chamber and to the door Pantiquod had left through. She eased it open, but it shrieked at her, and she found herself confronting the mad eyes of the little thrilpat, shut in with the Ghoul and dying on the floor.

"Harrah?" from the bed. "Who's there? Come into the light, you vermin."

She did not wait, but oozed through the crack and pulled it shut behind her, hearing the whisper, "Run, run, run," as she ran indeed, down the long way which arched into emptiness before her. What she had heard had been enough to give her an idea. Now she had only to find the place the shadowpeople were kept. After all, had not the Fon told her to do some service for them? What better service than to save them from this place?

Which was easier thought of than accomplished. Pantiquod walked for a great distance, through balconies

which stretched over vast audience halls, down twisting corridors, up curved flights of stairs and down similar ones, but at the end of it she came only to a wing
of the place devoted to suites of ordinary rooms, small
kitchens, servants' quarters, more luxuriously furnished
bedrooms and sitting rooms among them. Here there
was a certain amount of coming and going, and Mavin's
journey was interrupted by the constant need to hide.
After the fifth or sixth such occasion, she decided that
too much time was being wasted. It took only a little
creeping and spying to see what livery the servants of the
place wore, and then only a brief time more of experi-
mentation to shift into that livery and guise. Thereafter
she walked as a servant, obsequious and quiet, so ordinary about the face as to be anonymous. Pantiquod
entered a set of rooms which were evidently set aside for
her use, and did not emerge from them. She was obviously alone, and there was nothing Mavin could over-
hear or oversee to her advantage.

Well then, one must risk something. She returned the
way she had come, stopping at the first large hall in
which there was any appreciable traffic. "I have taken a
wrong turning," she said to an approaching servant. "I
was told by the woman, Pantiquod, to carry a message
to the guard of the chambers . . . below. Where the
shadowpeople are."

The servant stopped, stared, at last opened his mouth
to show a tongueless cavity there. Mavin's first reaction
was to run, or to vomit. She restrained herself, however,
and grasped the man firmly by one shoulder. "Do you
understand what I say?"

He nodded, terrified.

"Do you know the place, the door?"

He nodded again.

"Then lead me there. You may return here and none
know the difference."

Still fearful, shivering, the man set out at a run, Mavin striding alongside. They twisted, turned, then the man stopped just before coming to a corner and pointed around it, keeping well back, face white and contorted. Though she had no Demon's talent for reading minds, his was easy to read. "You were down there? That's where they cut out your tongue? I understand. Go." And he scurried back the way they had come, in such frantic haste that he stumbled, almost falling.

Mavin lay down upon the floor, peeked around the corner from floor level. At the end of the hallway was another of the guarded grills like those at the tunnel entrance to Hell's Maw. Before this gate, however, was no casual assembly of guardsmen but an armed line of Armigers, shoulder to shoulder, naked swords gleaming in their hands, a line of lounging Sorcerers behind them, blazing with power in that silent place.

"Oh, pombi piss," she muttered. "Filth and rot and foul disaster." Then she simply lay against the wall, exhausted, unable to think what to do next. How long had it been since she had had anything to eat? How long since she had slept? Probably a full day. They had had breakfast the day they entered Pfarb Durim. She had not eaten after that. Nor slept. She sighed. Well enough to know the way into the dungeons, but no help if one were too weak to go there. "Food," she murmured. "Food first. Then whatever comes next."

Chapter 7

She cursed herself tiredly for not having brought the food which Windlow had offered. What food she might find here in the depths of Hell's Maw had little likelihood of being healthful. "You are too rash, my girl," she lectured herself in silence. "You have done well so far, but what have you had to oppose you? A few old lechers in Danderbat keep, that's all. Now, here you are, run off in a sudden frenzy without any thought at all." Sighing, she rose and went skulking off in search of something to fill her empty belly.

The woman Pantiquod had looked more or less normal, that is, unghoulish, and she had seemed to live in a part of the caves and tunnels which was cleanly, not smelling of rot and mold. Mavin returned there, staying out of sight, poking about until she found a larder with fruit in it and loaves of bread smelling of the sun. Evidently not all those who lived in Hell's Maw were of Blourbast's persuasion. Perhaps only a few were, or none except the Ghoul himself. She wondered what diet the arrogant Huld had eaten, whether he had been cossetted with dainties from Pfarb Durim or fed from childhood on the horrors of the pit. None of this wondering did anything to destroy her appetite, which was ravenous. The tunnels were chill, and her shifting had drawn what power she carried with her, leaving her weary and weak. After a short rest, she began to feel stronger. "Able to shift for yourself again, girl," she said. "Able to shift." She created a capacious pocket to carry some of the food with her, knowing it might well be a long time before she would find more. She thought longingly of sleep, then rejected the idea. There was no time, not with Mertyn lying sick in Pfarb Durim and the image of Blourbast's ravaged face before her as a threat. Mertyn might come to this if she did not find help for him.

When she returned to the guarded hall it was to find the entrance to the lower realms unchanged. The line of Armigers still stood shoulder to shoulder; the Sorcerers behind them still lounged against the wall. They seemed not to have moved while she had been gone, as though some power she could not sense kept them in that utter stillness and concentration, entranced to their duty. It did no good to speculate. She had to get past them, preferably without alerting the warren to her presence.

Nothing came to her. She peered down the sides of the corridor, searching for any gap in the line. There was none. None. Except above the guardsmen's heads where the corridor arched into gloom above the glare of the shaded lanterns. Stretching from side to side below the vaulted ceiling was a line of wooden beams which tied the walls together, knobby and convoluted in the shadow, for they had been carved into likenesses of thick vines and bulbous fruits with pendant sprays of leaves fanning across the stone walls at either end. She examined them, then began to thin herself, to flow upward, to draw in upon herself while stretching out, becoming limbless, earless, hairless, softly scaled and quiet as a dream, relentlessly pouring up and onto the beam where she twisted about it in a bulky knot no different in outline from the carved vines.

The beam on which she rested was in the cross corridor. Now her serpent's head reached out into the guarded corridor, hidden in the gloom above the light, weaving out a little, silent, silent, until it rested on the next beam and anchored there. A long loop of body followed, knotting and unknotting slowly, moving forward as the sinuous body bridged the shadowy space, beam by beam. At last she lay above the guardsmen, twined onto the last of the beams, her endless neck reaching into the shadow behind them, over the Sorcerers' heads. There was nothing to hold her there except the lintel of the arch itself, and she descended by tiny tentacles sent deep into the mortar between the stones, holding herself to the wall as a vine holds, pulled tight to the rock until her serpent's head could pass through the iron grill, fingerlength by fingerlength. She lay at last beyond the grill and behind the guards, they not having moved during all that time. When the last scale of her tail slipped through the grill, her head was halfway down the flight of stairs behind, body stretched between the two points like a single reaching arm.

Now she heard again the sounds she had heard on first entering Hell's Maw, the clangor, the heavy pounding, the fragment of birdlike song, cut off abruptly. The stairs wound around a pit, down onto the floor of a well from which more of the arched corridors spread in all directions. The place was lit by the omnipresent torches. There were torches and lanterns everywhere in Hell's Maw, an insufficiency of light in all those depths, a gelid half shade thick with fumes and smoke. After a time she had stopped noticing the light, had only moved through its dusky inadequacy like a fish moving through water, not noticing the medium. Now, however, as she came to the bottom of the well, she saw that one of the tunnels to her left was lit in a stranger way, by a flickering which receded and advanced, receded and advanced, accompanied by a sound as of clattering wooden twigs upon stone. She started toward this way, then stopped as a stench poured out of the tunnel toward her, an effluvium so dense as to seem impenetrable. The wisp of birdlike sound came from behind her, and she turned, seeking the sound, finding any excuse not to go toward that flickering light.

Song led her into a darker way, one smelling of soil, but a cleaner stench than the corruption behind her. Roots dangled through the ceiling stones, brushes of dense hairy fiber dragging across the lean furred form she had taken. Snakes were all very well, she told herself, but stone was cold upon belly scales and the placement of the eyes left something to be desired. A twitter sounded ahead, and she melted into the darkness behind a pillar, searching. Nothing. No, perhaps a tiny movement. A scampering. Song again, a single, disconsolate trill. Then again. Silence. She snaked out a lengthened arm and grabbed into the gloom, then bit back a howl as needle teeth sank into her hand. Fighting down her instinct to drop whatever it was and run, Mavin toughened the flesh around the small thing she had caught and dragged it into the half light.

To stare in wonder, for it was like nothing she had ever seen before. Huge, fragile ears; wide lipless mouth; large dark eyes wild with fury and fear; teeth bared, slender form fluffed with soft fur, crying, crying words . . . words. She knew in an instant that it was no mere animal she held. The eyes, while frantic, were full of alert intelligence, and the sounds were too consecutive, too varied to be mere animal cries of panic. She sat down on the chill stone and crooned to it, without thinking, using the same tone she had used to Mertyn when he had hurt himself. "Ahh, ahh, it's all right. I won't hurt you. Shh. Shh. See, I'll hardly hold you at all. Now, who are you?"

She asked the question with an interrogative lilt and a cock of her head, waiting for an answer. The little creature stopped shaking and regarded her quietly, chest heaving with enormous sobs, quieting until only an occasional tremor ran through the muscular limbs she held so gently. "Mavin," she used one hand to point at herself. "Mavin." Then she pointed to her captive and cocked her head once more. "Who?"

"Puh-leedle-addle-proom-room-room," it warbled. "Puh-leedle-addle-proom-room-room."

Mavin shook her head, laughing. "Proom!" she pointed to him, relaxing her grip. "Mavin. Proom." This matter settled, she sat with the manikin on her lap, wondering what to do next. A final, sobbing breath passed through the creature, then it collapsed into her lap, sighing, such a sigh of despair and sadness as she had never heard. "What's the matter, little one?" she asked. "Are you as lost in this terrible place as I am?"

Proom tilted his head—Mavin was sure it was a "he," though she could not have said why—and thought about this for a moment. Then he reached up to lay one slender, three-fingered hand across her lips. The other he held behind his ear, the delicate pink nails curved above it. More clearly than with words he said, be still and listen. Then he sang, birdlike, a clear warble of sound in the ponderous dusk of the cavern. Mavin held her breath. She thought she heard a reply, or was it only an echo? No, it was a reply, for Proom's hand whipped away from her ear to point into the dark. A reply. There were others here, others in this place, and she knew already that they were not here by chance.

Something tickled at her mind, fled away.

Proom started to leap away, but she held him, placing him on her shoulder as she stood and moved in the direction he indicated. "I'll help you," she said, forgetting everything for the moment except the longing and despair in the little one's voice. "This way?" And she strode into the darkness. Torches were fewer along this way, but she compensated for the lack of light by making her eyes larger, her ears wider, not noticing Proom's astonishment at this, nor his obvious interest as she brought her reaching arms back to a more normal length.

"Andibar, bar, bar," he murmured.

She paid no attention. She was busy listening. They came to a fork in the way and she paused, looking to Proom for guidance. He warbled again, and again she heard a ghostly reply, thin, almost directionless, but Proom seemed to have no trouble knowing where it had come from, for he pointed down one of the branching ways without hesitation. They went on in this way, turn after turn, branch after branch, until Mavin had lost all sense of direction or place. Still, the answering voice grew more distinct each time they turned, and Proom's excitement was manifest as they went into the almost total dark. So it was Mavin almost impaled herself upon the spiked gate before she saw it. It was another of the ubiquitous grilled gates, this one with a mesh so small even a creature the size of Proom could not get through. He had pressed himself against it with a piteous cry, fingers thrust through the mesh as though he would pull himself through by an act of will. She knew he had been this far before. His despair could mean nothing else.

"Shh, shh," she said, tugging him away. Pressing herself against the mesh, making her eyes wide to gain all the available light, she could see the latch, high inside the gate. "Nothing to it," she murmured to the little one. "Nothing at all." A finger extended into a tentacle which wove its boneless way through the mesh, pushed upward and outward until the latch opened with a satisfying *tlock*. At first the gate would not move, but then as she threw her full weight against it, it screamed at her and sagged open on rusty hinges. Mavin stopped pushing to listen. Proom pushed past her and ran on down the corridor, the quick birdsong running before him in greeting. This time she heard the answer clearly, no mistake about it and no confusing echoes. Whoever sang in reply sang close before them.

She followed the sound, the two sounds, call and reply, as they grew louder, rounding a dim corner to find herself in a room hung with cages like that one which had held the unfortunate thrilpat, cages hung high on slender chains. They were out of reach of little Proom, no matter how he jumped and warbled to reach his imprisoned kin, and all the cavernous room thrilled with their birdsong twittering until Mavin was dizzy with it.

The song was interrupted by a monstrous clanging, as though from a gong unimaginably huge. All the little people writhed in pain on the bottom of their cages, tiny hands clamped across their ears. The clanging stopped, but the little creatures still cowered, sobbing, Proom also from his place on the stones. From some distance came a burst of evil laughter and the word "Silence . . ." shouted in a great voice. Then there was quiet, broken only by despairing whimpers from dozens of throats.

Mavin, at first confused by the noise, was now angry. Without stopping to think about it she began to stork upward, taller and thinner, so that she teetered to the height of the cages, then above them where they were fastened to rings in the high ceiling. She began to lower them, one, two, a dozen, twenty. Some of the cages held only one of Proom's people while others held two or three. She let them all down into the troubled quiet, and Proom gathered himself up to move among the cages, whispering, gesturing. He tugged at her ankle, pointing high where the ring of keys hung, and she passed them down to him, almost falling, for she had forgotten what a stiltwalker she had become. She folded into herself, suddenly weak and wan, aware that she had used up her strength and power again, depleted as it was in this chill place. She fished a piece of fruit from her pocket, bit into it, then saw some dozens pairs of eyes focused hungrily upon her. She gave them the other food she carried, watched with amazement as each creature took a single bite before passing it on. The food circled quickly, came back to her to be urged upon her again. She took her single bite and gave it back once more. Proom climbed into her lap and patted her on the head. "Mavin," he said. "Mavin, vin, vin."

"Introductions are all very nice," she said, "but I assume what you really want is to get out of here." She staggered to her feet and went back into the corridor, turning the way they had come. At once a dozen hands patted at her, pushing her in the opposite direction. Proom chattered, sniffed at the air, then agreed, following the others in their scamper toward a break in the corridor wall, thence into root-hung tunnels, and finally between two great knobbly tree roots into a rocky cavern of a different kind. Sunlight came upon them from above, the warm amber light of a distant afternoon. Around them hung icicles of stone, bulging buttresses of rock, walls of ochre and red and a long, straight path leading upward into leafy forests. She found strength she did not know she had to follow them up and out into a clearing among great trees. On a distant hill she could see the bulk of Pfarb Durim rising beyond its walls.

"Ahh?" called the little ones. "Ahh? Ahh?" They looked around, jigged uncertainly, called again and again, in some distress. It was obvious they did not know where they were. They had smelled their way out, but could not identify this location. Mavin hoisted Proom high on her shoulder where he could see the city through the trees. "Durim, rim, rim," he called, leaning down to give a hand up to others of his kindred. Mavin staggered under the load as twenty of them climbed her like a tree. There was pointing, argument, finally agreement, and most of the burden dropped away and vanished in the brush. Proom waited with her, regarding her with thoughtful eyes. After a time he beckoned, vanishing like the others in the shadow of the trees. The answer came then, simply, as if she had known it for some time. "Shadowpeople," disbelieving, yet knowing it was so. "These are the shadowpeople, and I have already done as the Fon suggested. I have done them a service. Now, shall I follow to see if they will do one for me?"

They traveled for a time in an arc, a long, curving line which kept Pfarb Durim always visible, high on its cliffs to their left. Once Mavin heard water, the sound of a considerable flow, making her believe that the River Haws ran no great distance from them in the forest. Others came back to them from time to time, bringing nuts and fruit and loaves of bread. Others came with messages, after some of which they changed direction. Mavin followed, uncomplaining, telling herself that now was a time for patience, for waiting to see what might happen next of its own accord, without her intervention. This patience was about to be exhausted when they arrived. The place of assembly was a hollow in the woods with a straight, tall tree at one side. The shadowpeople were gathered near it, staring upward. Mavin could see nothing from where she stood except a lumpish blob hanging high among the branches, swaying a little in the wind.

"Agirul," the shadowmen sang, dancing below the tree with its pendant form, swaying their bodies in time to the swaying of whatever it was above them. "Agirul, rul, rul."

Slowly, so slowly that she was not sure she saw it move at all, the lump turned its head over so that it faced downward, showing a tiny, three-cornered mouth, a shiny, licked-looking nose, two dark lines behind which eyes might be hiding. The mouth opened. "Ahhh, shuuuush," it said with great finality. "Shuuuush."

"Ahh shuuuush," sang the shadowmen, laughing, falling down in their laughter. Several of them ran off into the forest to return bearing slender bundles of long grass, the top of each stem tassled like a feather. They began to splice these together, making long, fragile lengths with which they tried to tickle the pendant creature, fluttering the tassled ends around its invisible ears, over its hidden eyes. One shadowman, more venturesome or inventive than the rest, concentrated his attention on the creature's rear, evidently touching some sensitive spot for the creature opened its tiny mouth once more and roared.

At this sound every one of the shadowpeople, down to the smallest cub, sat down at once with expressions of severity and solemnity sitting awkwardly upon their cheerful faces. Above them the creature went on roaring as it swung to the trunk of the tree and began to descend, ponderously, long leg after long arm, like a pendulum swinging on its way downward, tic by toc, to slump at last on the ground at the roots of the tree, long legs and arms sprawled wide and helpless. It began to draw itself into some more coordinated posture, and two of the shadowpeople ran to help, murmuring, patting, easing the creature onto its haunches with its monstrously long arms folded neatly into its lap.

"Naiii shuuush," it complained, scratching its head with two curved nails, "Mumph, mumph, who is this person?"

A warbled answer came from the assembly. The beast considered, then turned its head to Mavin.

"I suppose you'll insist that this wasn't your idea," it bellowed at her in a petulant voice. "The little beasts won't let me alone."

"No—it was not my idea. Not letting you alone, I mean. Since I didn't know that you exist, I could hardly . . ."

"No. No, of course not. No one has any idea, not ever. Don't they teach languages in the benighted schools you people attend? Why shouldn't you learn to speak shadow-talk? Why shouldn't they speak whatever ugly tongue we are speaking now? But no. No, it's always come to Agirul for translation, because that's easier. Shush. Get away, you," and it pushed ineffectually at the crowd of shadowpeople who were still busy propping it up and cushioning its back with leafy twigs. It did not look comfortable. Its arms and legs were not designed for living on the ground, sprawling uncontrolled as though the muscles would not work out of the trees. One look at its hands told Mavin that it was a tree liver which never came to the ground of its own will, for it had curved hooks of bone growing from each palm.

"They didn't hurt you, did they?" she asked.

"Of course they didn't hurt me. They woke me! They know I dislike being wakened. It has been sleeping weather recently, good sleeping weather, and I hate having it interrupted. I'm not unwilling to accede to emergency, however, and these little people always seem to have one. I suppose it's you they want to talk with?"

Mavin cast a wondering glance around. "I suppose so. I helped them get out of Hell's Maw. I want to talk to them, very much. I need their help."

The Agirul sighed. "Hell's Maw. Blourbast the Ghoul. I heard he had ghoul-plague. Why isn't he dead?"

"I don't know. He looks half dead. His hands and face are covered with sores, but he claims he will recover. Does it always kill? The plague, I mean?"

"Obviously not always. Ah, you brighten at that? It means something to you that some recover? Well, we will explore the notion soon. Just now it seems that Proom is ready to explain why I was awakened."

There was a brief colloquy, then the Agirul murmured to Mavin that it would attempt to make a simultaneous translation of the explanation which was about to follow. "Woman, it may be you will understand nothing at all, in which case I will explain when they have finished. It is the desire of Proom that you be honored by a song—and since his people are quite decent in the matter of gifts, fruits, you know, and nuts, and even a bit of roast meat from time to time—I will accommodate them. Sit comfortably now, this may take some time."

The hooked hand drew her gently close, and she squirmed about until her head lay near the Agirul's mouth. For a moment, she feared she would go to sleep, thus disgracing herself, but once the singing started, she did not think of sleep again.

"*Hear the song of Proom!*" It was a solo voice which sang this phrase, each syllable dropped into the clearing as a stone may be dropped into still water. The echoes of it ran in ripples across the gathered faces, gathering force, returning from the edges to the center amplified. Agirul murmured the words, but she did not hear the

words, only the song. When the echoes had died, the
voice sang again.

> "Summoned, Proom, by those who live forever.
> Summoned, Proom, on a great journey.
> Far to go. Many seasons spent. Doubt shall he
>   return.
> Ah, Proom, Proom, keeper of Ganver's Bone."

Now those gathered in the clearing took up the song, a
full chorus. Some of these little ones had deeper voices
than she had heard before, and these deeper voices set
up a drone beneath the song, dragging, ominous.

> "Shall the Bone go? Far from the people?
> Shall the Bone travel far from its own place?
> Shall the Bone depart from Ganver who gave it?"

Three voices sang alone, joined by flutes and bells.

> "Leave the Bone, Proom, before answering the
>   summons.
> Leave the holy thing among its people.
> If Proom does not return, the Bone remains."

Now there were drums, little and big, cymbals ringing,
and a solo voice, awe filled, chanting.

> "Now see, listen all, Proom left it in the high place.
> In the sacred place. Forbidden place. Guarded place.
> Farewell, Proom. Go with song around you."

Now a solo drum, high-pitched, frenetic, full of panic,
one voice, very agitated.

> "See who comes. Blourbast the Ghoul.
> Riding.
> Riding.
> Blourbast does not see the things which guard.
> Blourbast does not feel forbidden place.
> Blourbast cannot tell sacred from his excrement hole."

Full chorus once again, full of wrath.

> "The Ghoul sees it.
> The Ghoul takes it.

    Ganver's Bone, Bone, Bone,
    Gone, gone, gone, alas.''
Now the voices lamented, high, keening.
    "Terror, terror, monstrous this evil.
    The holy thing lost in dreadful's hands.
    One must go recover what is lost.''
Now drums, fifes, cymbals clashing, something that
sounded suspiciously like a trumpet, though Mavin
thought it was a voice.
    "Come to the place, the evil place.
    Call out for the return of Ganver's Bone!''
Now an old, old female rose, her voice a whispery chant
in the clearing, barely heard over the humming of the
multitude.
    "Comes one from Hell's Maw,
    An old, gray man,
    Servant of Blourbast.
    Lo, he sings the words of Blourbast.
    Lo, he sings them in the people's song.
    'Let twelve of the people come or Ganver's
      Bone will be destroyed!' ''
Now a quartet of strong voices, in harmony.
  "Ah, ah, Proom, thou art far away. Ah. Ah.
  Aloom is old, is sick, Aloom sings.
  "I will go, I will go, that Ganver's Bone shall never
    be destroyed.''
  Aloom goes, and behind her others go.
  Twelve gone. Old ones, sick ones, twelve gone.
  This is one time.
  Time passes.''
There was a moment's silence, then the voices went on.
  "The old, gray man sang once more, 'Let twelve
    come.
  Ah, ah, Proom, thou art far away. Ah. Ah.
  Duvoon is quiet, is loving, Duvoon sings.

'I will go, I will go, that Ganver's Bone shall never
        be destroyed.'
Duvoon goes, and behind him others go.
Twelve gone. Male ones, female ones, twelve gone.
This is two times.
Time passes.''

Again silence, again the voices.

''The old, gray man sang once more, 'Let twelve
        come.'
Ah, ah, Proom, thou art far away. Ah. Ah.
Shoomdu is Proom's child. Shoomdu sings.
''I will go, I will go, that Ganver's Bone shall never
        be destroyed.''
Shoomdu goes, and behind her others go.
Twelve gone. Children ones, little ones.
This is three times.
Time passes.''

Now the chorus again, ugly in wrath, full of fury,
quickly, almost shouting.

''Oh, behold, plague comes on Blourbast.
Oh, behold, Ghoul has eaten our flesh.
Oh, behold, he is maddened, he kills the old gray
        man.
Oh, behold, Proom, Proom, Proom returns.''

Hearing his name sung, Proom stood up and began to
chant, waving his arms high, leading the chorus and the
drums.

''Hear the song of Proom, Voice of the Songmakers.
'No more shall go to Hell's Maw.
All who went shall come again to us if yet they live.
Holy Ganver will forgive us this.'
Hear the song of Proom, 'I will go in.' ''

''Daroo, roo, roo,'' sang the multitude. ''Daroo, roo,
roo, pandillio lallo lie, daroo.''

''So he went, wandered, wandered, wandered,

in the dark, the smell, the pain,
Lost, he wandered into the very hands of her
Mavin who takes many forms.
Now of her we sing.
Now we sing the song of Mavin.''

"I suggest you make yourself comfortable," said the Agirul. "They are about to begin singing."

"Gamelords," whispered Mavin. "What do you call what they have been doing?"

"Oh, that was just getting warmed up," it replied. "They have sung their song. Now they will sing the song of Mavin who . . . "

"Mavin Manyshaped," she said to the beast. "Mavin Manyshaped." He did not hear her. The chorus was already in full cry.

Afterwards, Mavin supposed it had been a kind of enchantment. Certainly while it was going on there was nothing she could do about it or herself. She was the center of a whirlpool of song, drawn down into it, drowned in it, surfacing at last with a feeling that some heavy, nonessential part of her had been washed away leaving her as light and agile as the shadowpeople themselves. When they had finished their song, they went away into the forest, leaving only a few behind.

"I could translate for you the words of the song they have just sung, Mavin Manyshaped, but the words do not matter." The Agirul nodded to itself. "They have made a song of you, and that is what matters, for they do not make songs of every little happening or every chance encounter. Quite frankly, I do not know why they have honored you in this way. You were at little risk of your life in that place, so far as I can tell. Whatever their reason, you are now brought into their history, and your song will be sung at the great convocations on the high places until you are known to all the tribes wherever they may be. You may call upon the people for help, and they will be with you in your times of need.

"I trust that now I may be allowed to go back to sleep." And with that, the Agirul turned to begin climbing back up the tree.

Mavin cried out, "No. Don't go. I came for a reason, Agirul. I have need now. I must talk to them."

Proom had heard the tone of her voice, and he came to her with brow furrowed. Mavin reached out to him even as she began speaking, hastily, words tumbling over one another. "Mertyn," she said. "Brother . . . sick . . . woman said shadowpeople . . . cure . . . graywoman . . . Pantiquod . . ."

"Hush," said Agirul. "Start again. Slowly. What is the trouble?"

So she began again, telling it more slowly, giving Agirul time between thoughts to translate her meaning. Proom's face changed, gave way to horror, then despair. When Mavin said that Mertyn lay ill with ghoul-plague, he cried out, tearing at his fur with both hands. Others ran toward him, questions trilling on their tongues, only to begin keening when he explained.

"What is it?" cried Mavin. "What's the matter?"

Agirul shook its narrow head. "Mavin Manyshaped, you have come on a fruitless quest. The disease you speak of is one which long ago took great toll of their lives. Then came Ganver, Ganver the Great, Ganver of the Eesties, to tell the people he would give them a gift in return for a song. So they made a song for Ganver, and he gave them his Bone. It is only by using the Bone they may cure the illness, and the Bone is gone—gone down there, in Blourbast's hands, where you may have seen it yourself."

"Is that the thing Blourbast took? The thing he wears

around his neck? The thing he was holding for ransom?''

"It is. And Proom believes that when Blourbast found the shadowpeople had escaped, he probably destroyed the Bone as he threatened to do. Proom says he could not leave his people, his own child, to be eaten, not even for Ganver's Bone, but now he is unable to repay his debt to Mavin Manyshaped. He says he will kill himself at once.''

"No!'' she shrieked. "Tell him no. Mavin forbids it. Ganver forbids it. Tell him whoever forbids it so that he won't do it. That's terrible. Oh, Gamelords, what a mess.''

She set herself to think. It did not come easily. There was too much in her head, too many squirming thoughts, Blourbast and Pantiquod, the caverns below, the flickering lights and horrible smells, Pfarb Durim high on the cliff surrounded by the host, the song of the little people, the face of Agirul. Too much. "I want the Fon,'' she said, not even knowing she had said it.

"The Fon?'' asked Agirul.

"A Wizard. But he's shut up in Pfarb Durim, so even if I sent the message we agreed upon, it would do no good.''

"A Wizard? I would not be too sure about that. If I were you, I would send the message and leave it to the Wizard to decide whether it will do any good or not. Is there not a saying among your people? 'Strange are the Talents of Wizards?' What was the message?''

"The letter M, in any form, set so he could see it.''

"Well then. Dark comes soon. We will send him a message he cannot fail to see.''

Though she fumed at the delay, she could think of nothing else to do. She had not slept since leaving Pfarb Durim, and when the Agirul suggested she do so, and when Proom's people made her a leafy nest cradled in the roots of a great tree, she told herself that she would need to sleep sooner or later, so it might as well be done now. Though she was sure worry would keep her awake, the shadowpeople were singing a slow, calm song which reminded her of wind, or water running over stones, and she sank into sleep to the sound of it as though she had been drugged. She went down and down into dreamless black, and did not come up until the stars shone on her through windwoven trees.

"Be still," said the Agirul from a branch above her. "Look through the trees to your right."

She sat up, stretching, seeing through the branches a long slope of meadow on which dozens of tiny fires burned in long lines.

"You cannot see it from where you are," the lazy voice from above her mused, "but the fires make your name letter on a slope which faces the city. They have been burning since dusk, half a night's length. The shadowpeople have been bustling about dragging branches out of the forest for hours. They will keep the fires alight until dawn."

"No need," said a firm voice from the trees. "They may let the fires die."

"Twizzledale!" cried Mavin. "How did you get out? How did you find me? How . . . "

"Ah," as he came silently across the grass, a moving blackness across the burning stars, "it took much longer than it should have done. However, when I went to one of the watchtowers, I found that the watchmen had gone—for tea, perhaps, or to quell some disturbance in the city. They had left a rope ladder there, useful for climbing down walls."

"But the armies? The besiegers?"

"Evidently there had been some attempt to leave the city by some half-score merchants, and a group of the besiegers had gone to drive them back, leaving the road unguarded. Quite coincidental, of course, but for-tuitous. . . ."

"Fortuitous," murmured the Agirul. "Coinci-dental."

"Whom have I the honor of addressing?" asked the Fon in measured tones, as though he were a Herald preparing to announce Game.

"The Agirul hangs in the trees above you," said Mavin. "It is a translator of languages. The shadow-people wakened it so that they might talk with me."

"And kept me awake," said Agirul in an aggrieved tone. "I will not catch up on my sleep for a season or more."

"I have great honor in speaking with you," said the Fon, "though I would not have wished your discomfort for any purpose of my own convenience. . . ."

The Agirul tittered. "Wizards. They all talk like that. Unless they are involved in some Game or other." The titter turned into a gurgle, then into a half snore.

"Well, Mavin," said the Fon, seating himself close beside her in the nest. "What have you been up to?"

As she spoke, the fires died. Proom returned to sit beside them, ashy and disconsolate. The Agirul was roused from time to time to ask a question or translate a response. Night wore on and the stars wheeled above them, in and out of the leaves like lantern bugs. At last the Fon had asked every question which could be asked and had set to brewing tea over a handful of coals, hum-ming to himself as he did so. Proom crouched by the fire, humming a descant, and soon a full dozen of the shadowpeople were gathered at the fire in full con-trapuntal hum, which seemed to disturb the Fon not at all. When he had the tea brewed to his satisfaction, he shared a cup round with them then brought a full one to share with Mavin.

"Blourbast has not destroyed the Bone," he said.

Over his head, Agirul murmured, and a sigh went round the fire.

"He would not. He would think that a thing held in such reverence by the shadowpeople must be a thing of power or value. Blourbast would not destroy anything which might be a source of power. He is vicious, wantonly cruel, irredeemably depraved, but he is not stupid. He would not discard a thing of value merely to avenge himself upon those he despises. He would keep it, study it, perhaps even seek out those who might know of such things. Now I have heard of Eesties, as have we all. Myths, I thought. Legends. Stories out of olden time. This thing, whatever it may be, whether Eesty bone or artifact or some natural thing, must be obtained if we are to work a cure upon your brother and the others who lie ill and dying in Pfarb Durim. There are some hundred of them in the city. Mertyn is no worse than he was, but he is no better either. So a cure is needed, and if not for him then for the others. The Healers will not relent. Heralds have been sent to them—even Ambassadors, with promises of magnificent gifts—but they stand adamant. Until Blourbast is dead they will bring no healing to Pfarb Durim."

"Why?" cried Mavin. "Pfarb Durim is not Hell's Maw. Why hold the city ransom for what Blourbast has done?"

"Because the city profits from what Blourbast does," replied Twizzledale. "It stands aloof, pretends it does not share in Blourbast's depravity, murmurs repudiation of his horrors, but sells to Hell's Maw what Hell's Maw buys and takes in return the coin Blourbast has stolen or extorted or melted out of the bones of those he eats. The Healers lay guilt where guilt is due. No. Pfarb Durim is not innocent, nor are those who trade there innocent."

"And we," mumbled Mavin, white-lipped, "we who

came there unknowing, but still spent our coin on lodging, on food? Are we guilty?''

The Fon shook his head, smiling, reached out to touch her face—then thought better of it, for she was close to tears. "Mavin, did you know of all this before entering the city? Well, neither did I, nor Windlow either. I do not hold us guilty of anything but ignorance, though we will be guilty indeed if we come this way again or buy anything which comes from Pfarb Durim. Enough of this conscience searching. We must find this thing, this Bone.''

"Blourbast had a thing around his neck, something long and white, which he stroked. He spoke of it to that woman, his sister, stroking it with his awful-looking hand, covered with sores. She wore a kind of cap with birds wings at the side, and there were feathers on her shoulders. I don't know what Talent she has. . . .''

"Harpy," he replied. "His sister, a Harpy, mother of that Huld whom we so much enjoyed meeting. Not only Blourbast's sister, seemingly, but his emissary as well. She who arranged for the plague to be spread in the city. Did she assume herself immune?''

"Probably she was simply careful not to touch anything, not to become infected. But Blourbast thought himself immune. Even now he thinks he will recover.''

"Perhaps," mused the Fon while the Agirul translated what they said to the shadowpeople amid much twittering and warbling. "And perhaps he only blusters. If what you say is true, however, if he wears it upon him, touches it, then we may not think of your going to fetch it. You would become ill and we would be no better off. No, we must get him to bring it out—find a way to use it without touching it. . . .''

The Wizard got up to stride to and fro, rooting his hair up into spiky locks with both hands, as though he dug in his brain for answers he could not find. "He sought to compel healing from the shadowpeople, what would happen it were offered to him? Can Proom tell us in what way the Bone is used in preparing the cure?" He waited for the usual twittering exchange before the beast replied in a sleepy voice.

"It is a matter of music, Wizard. One note of which is summoned from Ganver's Bone."

"Need the Bone be in Proom's hands? Could any person holding it summon the note as needed?"

This time there was a lengthy colloquy, argument, expostulation, before the beast said, "Proom acknowledges that the note could be struck by any. He denies that any has that right except himself, but it is not a matter of impossibility."

"Ah," said the Fon with satisfaction, "Then, then . . . " And his hands waved as he sketched a plan, improvising, leaping from one point to the next as the Agirul muttered along and Mavin watched in fascination.

When he had finished, Mavin said, "But . . . but, your plans calls for several shifters. Three, four, more perhaps."

"That is true," he murmured. "No help for it. We must have them. Well, shifter girl? Have you no kin to call upon?"

"Danderbat keep, from which I came, is not within a day's travel," she replied. "I was traveling to Battlefox keep, somewhere in the Shadowmarches to the north. My thalan is there, and my kindred and Mertyn's. Is it within hours of travel? I do not know. Shall I run there seeking help which may arrive too late?"

The Agirul began its murmuring and twittering while the little people chattered and trilled. "Battlefox is within a few hours, Mavin," it said at last. "One or more of the people will go with you as your guide.''

The Fon was staring at the ground where his busy hands made drawings in the dust. At the edge of the world dawn crept into the sky. "When must it be done?" he asked of Proom. "What time of day or night?"

"In the deep of night," replied the beast. "When the blue star burns in the horns of Zanbee. Do I say that right?"

"You do." The Fon smiled. "Were you translating, or did you think of that yourself? It is an odd bit of esoterica for you to know. Well then, Mavin, you must return to that road south of Pfarb Durim which we have traveled once before. Beneath the Strange Monuments there, at midnight, we will find a cure. Come with whatever help you can muster. You do understand the plan?"

"As well as I may," she said distractedly, "having heard it only once. You will probably change it, too, as the day wears on. Nonetheless, I will do what I can. Do you, also, Fon, for my hope rests in you." She was very sober about this, and the tears in the corners of her eyes threatened to spill.

He took her hand in his to draw her up but then did not release her. Instead he pulled her tight to him. At first she struggled, fighting against the strength of his arms as she would have fought the constraints of a basket in Danderbat keep, full of panic and sudden fear. Then something within her weakened, perhaps broke, and she found herself pressed against his chest, hearing the throb of his heart beneath her ear, aware for the first time that he was seeing her, holding her, in her own shape, in her essential Mavin-ness. He did so only for a moment, then let her go with a whisper.

"Go, then. Trust in me so far as you may, Mavin. It

is your Wizard, Himaggery, who promises it after all.
Bring what help you can and we will put an end to this.''

She did not trust herself to say anything more, but
turned to run from him in that instant. From him, or in
order to return to him, but she did not really think of
that.

Chapter 8

"I run," she said between her teeth, putting one foot before another on her long-legged form, feeling the clutch of shadowperson knees behind her shoulders where the little creature rode astride, whooping its pleasure at the speed of their movement. "I run," concentrating on that, trying not to think of the plan the Fon—Himaggery—had sketched before them, vaporous now, too many details missing, too many things that could go wrong. "I run," chanting it like an incantation, moving in the direction the little heels kicked her, up long slopes under the leaves spangled with sun, out into green glades where flowers bloomed higher than her head, then into shade again and down, down into gullies where gnarled black branches brooded against the sky, making a cold shade over the wet moss. The way tended always upward, coming at last to a leg-stunning climb beside a tumbling fall of water, all white spray and wet, slick rock where ferns nodded in time to the splashes. "I run," she panted, trying to convince herself, making the back legs longer to kick herself up with and the front ones clawed to scratch at the slippery rock. It was not a run, more like a scrambling climb. At the top, however, the land leveled into long shadowy rides among the groves of sky-topped trees, and the little heels kicked her into a lope once more.

"Away northwest," the voice on her back trilled, and she needed no Agirul to translate the song. It sang of sky, tree, and direction, and she understood it in her bones. The shadows dwindled but it was still short of noon when she topped a long ridge to look downward upon Battlefox keep sprawled wide in the center of its p'natti. And here she was, come to Plandybast's place —not with a modest appeal for lodging and food, perhaps for friendship if kinship should not be enough. No, here she was to beg followers, warriors, fighters, shifters to shift for something they had probably not heard of and would not care for.

Well then. How did a shifter enter a keep? Or, how best might Mavin enter a keep to make such demands upon short acquaintance?

She urged the little one down from her back so that she might sit herself down, back against tree, to eat a bit and think. The shadowperson sat comfortably beside her, snuggled close for warmth, but making no protestations at the sight of the place before her. After all, she told herself, the creature had guided her here. It probably knew as much about the place as Mavin did. Once it trilled, but her hand stilled it, and it merely hummed quietly like a kettle boiling.

Suppose that Battlefox Demesne was not so hidebound as Danderbat keep. Still, they were shifters, full of shifterish Talent and seeming. Would they respect her need? Could they offer help where they did not respect? Could she ask from weakness what she could not demand from strength? How did Plandybast stand within the walls? Was he high up in the way of things, or a mere follower after? All in all, well—all in all, would it be better to do something shifterish and fail at it or to do nothing shifterish at all and leave them wondering? She chewed and ruminated, unable to make up her mind, wishing the Wizard were there to give her some firm instructions to take the doubt away.

Finally she swallowed, sighed, pointed firmly at the base of the tree where they sat and said to the shadow-person, "You stay here."

The little head cocked. A narrow hand was placed on the trunk of the tree, and a voice warbled, "Quirril?"

"I suppose," she said. "Quirril. Until I come back."

She stood long upon the hill, remembering the way Wurstery Wimpole had come into Danderbat Keep, the drumming, the rolling, launching, flying, slything down, then up once more into veils which fell as soft as down. She sighed. She had never flown, had no idea how. Serpent forms were easy, but those immediate transitions were something she had never practiced. Better not to try anything of the sort.

And there was always the she-road, cutting through the p'natti straight as a shadow line. But if Plandybast had been correct, then only pregnant women used that road coming into Battlefox. What to do, to do, to do?

"Well, girl," she said to herself. "What would you have done if you and Mertyn had come here as you planned? You'd have walked up to the gate in your own shape, holding Mertyn by the hand. For aren't you the thalani of Plandybast, and hasn't he invited you to come? There's no time for anything else, no time for making a show of yourself, so go, go, go." And before she could talk herself out of it or think of anything else to worry about, she stepped out into the light of the sun and began walking toward the keep.

The drum sounded when she was only halfway there. It boomed once, then once again, not in any panic

sound, more as a warning to let those in the keep know
that someone was on the road. She did not hurry,
merely kept walking, her eyes upon the walls. Forms
materialized there as she watched, dozens of them, still
as stone and as full of eyes as an oxroot. No sound. No
welcome, only those eyes. What were they looking at?
Nothing to see upon the road but one girl, dressed in
whatever old thing she had shaped around herself.
Mavin stopped suspiciously. They were entirely too
silent. She turned her head slowly. There, behind her,
was her guide—her guide and two or three dozen of his
kindred.

"Gamelords," she said. "What have I done now?"

The shadowperson who had ridden her shoulders so
happily came forward to take her dangling hand.
"Quirril?" it asked. "Quirril?"

For a moment she could not think what to do. Then
she shrugged and hoisted the little one onto her shoulders, beckoning the others to come on. "Come," she
cried aloud, "Let us visit my thalan, Plandybast."

She stopped within a few man-heights of the gate,
peering upward at the watchers along the wall.
"Plandybast," she cried, making her voice a trumpet,
full of sonority, dignified and pleading at once. "Plandybast, I come at your invitation, I, your sister's child,
Mavin." Then she waited, ready, so she told herself, for
someone to call down in a cold voice that Plandybast
was not at home, or had never lived here, or was long
dead.

Instead the gate began to creak, and she saw the
almost familiar face peering at her from around the corner. "Mavin? May I come out? Will I frighten them?
Some are saying they are . . . shadowpeople? Could that
be true?"

She wanted to giggle. All her worry and concern, and
here was her thalan as full of wonder as some child see-

ing Assembly for the first time. "Come out, Plandy-bast. I don't think they'll frighten, not so long as I am here."

He came to her, put his hand out to her, watching the little rider on her shoulder the while. "Where's Mertyn?" he asked. "What's happened?"

"Thalan, there is no time to tell you everything that has happened. I can only tell you two important things. Mertyn lies ill of ghoul-plague in Pfarb Durim. That is the first thing. The second is that a cure may be wrought by these little ones, if I bring some of my kindred to help. I need you, you and some others."

Plandybast looked up, called to the watchers, "It is as we heard. Ghoul-plague. In Pfarb Durim."

There was an immediate outcry, a kind of stifled protest or moan, and he turned back to her, shaking his head in a kind of fussy sympathy which hid his curiosity only a little.

"You must be frantic with worry," he said. "I can see that. You say there's little time? Surely you have time to come in? To eat a little something? Have a warming drink?"

She shook her head, looking sideways at the shadows, seeing how they stretched now a little east, a little past high noon. "We must be there by midnight. The Agirul said when the blue star burns in the horns of Zanbee. A Wizardly saying, evidently. Midnight. No later than that, and it is a way from here. As far as I have run since dawn, and farther. We must be there. Will some of you come, Plandybast? Do we have other kin here who will help us?"

"I will come with you if you need me, of course. But to ask others—we must at least tell them where. And what the plan may be. And why they are needed. They will be so curious, so delighted to see you. Can you come in?"

She moved toward the gate, a bit uneasily, at which all the assembled shadowpeople began to cry out, moving away from her, and her shoulder rider began to scramble down, bleating.

"They won't come in," she sighed. "They have no good experience of walls. If I come in, they may all go—and I need them to guide me back. No. Better I stay out here. Could you bring us something to eat? I had some food with me, but not enough. . . ."

"Don't distress yourself, child. Or them. This is so great a wonder, why should we spoil it with ordinary behavior. If they will not come in, we will come out." He called up to the watchers again, and there was a bustling among them as some went off at his request. It was not long before two or three of the shifters came out of the gate carrying baskets laden with fresh loaves split open and filled with roasted meat. There was no need for the shadowpeople to pass the food about or share it for each of them had both hands full. By that time a dozen of the Battlefox shifters had gathered at Plandybast's side, and Mavin found herself trying to explain once more.

There were long looks from the Battlefoxes. Long looks and pursed lips, shaken heads and skeptical eyes. Among the most doubtful-looking was one Itter, a narrow-faced woman introduced as Plandybast's sister —at which Plandybast merely looked uncomfortable, saying nothing to confirm or deny this claim. "Who is he?" the woman asked when Mavin spoke of the Fon.

"A Wizard," she replied for the third time. "From the southlands."

"A Wizard," the questioner repeated after her, making the words sound slick and unreliable. "From the south."

"Yes," Mavin said, beginning to be angry. Everything the woman said was an accusation, an allegation of dishonesty or stupidity, unspoken but most explicitly conveyed in her words. "A Wizard. A young Wizard. Perhaps too young to be much regarded by the dwellers of Battlefox. As I am young. As Mertyn, who will die if a cure is not found, is young." She clenched her fist, turning from them to her thalan who stood shifting from one foot to the other at the edge of the group. "It comes to that in the end, doesn't it, Plandybast? The Fon and I are young enough to need help, therefore too young to be trusted when we ask for it."

"Now, child," he objected, "don't be so quick with blame. Itter didn't mean to sound . . . "

"Oh, but I did," said Itter sweetly. "Your other sister, Plandybast, was known for her eccentricity, her individuality. Are we to assume that her child—her children—are any less . . . individual?" In the woman's mouth the word became a curse, an indictment.

"Now, now, no need to rake up old troubles. Let's take a little time to talk this out."

"There's no time!" Mavin cried. "Tonight it will be done. The little people will be there, and the Fon, and old Blourbast with his armies and his foul sister. And I am supposed to be there, too, with help from the shifter kindred. They will expect me, and I will not fail them no matter what the people of Battlefox do or don't do."

"Why not let the Ghoul alone?" the woman asked in her sharp, accusing voice. Her eyes were calculating and cold. Her mouth curved but her eyes were chilly, and the shadowperson cringed away from her when she stepped closer. "The Ghoul does no more than any Gamesman. He plays in accordance with his Talent. From what you say, the Wizard's plan will work well enough without shifters. The cure will be wrought. The people will be healed. What matter that the Ghoul returns to his tunnels? What business is it of ours? Our business is the education of our young, not interfering with Ghouls.

When he is cured, you bring Mertyn here to be educated, and forget the Ghoul. All will be as it was before.''

"But it will not be as it was before," said Mavin, gritting her teeth. She had already said this twice. "The disease is one which afflicts the shadowpeople from time to time. They have always been able to cure it before, with the Bone. If Blourbast is left alive, if he returns to his tunnels with the Bone, then the disease will strike again, and again. As it returned again and again in the ancient time." The little creature on her shoulder trilled, and Mavin understood the meaning. "My friend says it may strike next time at you, Madam Itter, and at the children you are so eager to see educated, perhaps your own. It would not be wise to return to that ancient time, before Ganver.''

Hearing this name the shadowpeople began to sing, a lamenting song, full of runs and aching sadness, so engaging a song that they put down the food they held to put their arms about one another and sway as they sang.

"What are they doing?" asked the woman in sudden apprehension.

"They sing of Ganver. A god to them. Perhaps Ganver would have been a god to us as well. It is Ganver's Bone the Ghoul has. Listen to them, woman! Listen to them, Plandybast! To you they were legends? Myths? Now they are here before you, singing, and you owl me with those doubtful eyes and will not promise to help me." She flung her arms wide in a despairing gesture and moved away from them toward the shadowpeople.

Plandybast came after her. "Some of them will probably come, Mavin. Just give them a little time. Itter is a kind of sister to me. At least, her mother said she was my father's child. But you've heard her. She always assumes that others are stupid, or evil, or both. It isn't only you, she behaves so to all of us. And she does have a point, you know. There seem to be a lot of details you're not sure of. And none of us relish the idea of having anything to do with the plague, or with the Ghoul, come to that. We don't really interfere in the business of the world that much, we Battlefoxes. Oh, we hire ourselves out for Game from time to time, but there seems to be no fee and no honor in this. . . ."

"Fee! Honor! I have seen these little ones so frightened that their faces run with tears and shuddering so hard with sobs they can scarcely stand, and they go on while they are crying! I call that honor, Plandybast. You would respond better to a call to Game? If I had come with a Herald, announcing challenge, would that have made it easier? I could have done that! Watch, now, thalan. See the Herald come?" She was angry and tired. She shifted without thinking as she had done once before in Danderbat keep, without planning it, letting her shape become that of the Herald she had seen outside the walls of Pfarb Durim. She made her voice a bugle, let it ring across the walls of Battlefox keep. "Give ear, oh people of Battlefox Demesne, for I come at the behest of the Wizard Himaggery, most wise, most puissant, to bring challenge to the sluggards of this keep that they stay within their walls while Game moves about them!" Then she trembled, and the shape fell away. There was only silence from them, and astonishment, and—fear.

"Impossible," Plandybast quavered. "Shifters cannot take the form of other Gamesmen. But your face was the face of the Herald Dumarch-don. I know him. Your voice was his voice. Impossible. You're only a child."

"I'm a forty-six-season child," she agreed. "It is said to be impossible, but I can do it. Sometimes. You have not asked how we escaped from Danderbat keep, thalan. You have not asked how I came out of Pfarb Durim, a city under siege. It is better, perhaps, that you do not know, but I made use of this Talent to do it. I have been long on the road to you, coming to you at your invitation. Now look to your kin. They are all fainting with shock." And she turned away bitterly, knowing that fear had done what politeness might have prevented—made them refuse to help her.

Itter was already cawing at the group, "You see! What did I tell you! She is no true shifter! Can a true shifter take the shape of other Gamesmen? Can they? I said her mother was guilty of individuality, and so she was. Now will you believe me?"

"Go with them," Mavin said wearily to Plandybast. "I will wait out here here for an hour, perhaps two. I will sleep here on this sun-warmed hill and make strength for the journey back, among my small friends who account themselves my kindred while my kindred sort out whether they are my friends or not. Any who will come with me will be welcome. If none will come —well, so be it." And she turned away from him to move into the welcoming arms of the shadowpeople who snuggled about her on the slope, a small hillock of eyes watching the walls of Battlefox Demesne.

A voice spoke calmly from above her head. "They are not eager in your aid, your kinsmen."

She looked up. The Agirul hung above her head. "How did you get here?" she cried. Around her the little people twittered and laughed.

"I have been here," said the Agirul. "All along."

"Then you're not . . . the one who . . . you don't know . . ."

"What the Agirul knows, the Agirul knows," said the creature in a voice of great complacency. "Which means all of it, wherever its parts may be." It released one long, clawed arm to scratch itself reflectively, coughing a little, then twittering a remark to the shadowpeople which made them all sigh. "I said that you are saddened by your reception in this place."

"Old Gormier would have been biting on the bit by now,"she said. "Him and Wurstery and the others. They may be evil old lechers, but they would have been full of fire and ready to move." Then she added, more honestly, "Of course, I don't really know that to be true. They might have been willing to be involved, but might not have responded to a plea from me, or Handbright, or any girl from behind the p'natti."

"Wisdom," growled the Agirul. "Painful, isn't it? We assume so much and resist learning to the contrary. Well, neither Danderbat nor Battlefox meets our needs at the moment. Shall we consider other alternatives?"

"Our needs, Agirul? I didn't know you were involved."

The beast swung, side to side, a furry pendulum, head weaving on its heavy neck. "Well, girl person, if we were to speak strictly of the matter, I am not involved. If we speak of curiosity, however, and of philosophy, and of being wakened and not allowed to go back to sleep —there are consequences of such things, wouldn't you agree? And consequence breeds consequence, dragging outsiders in and thrusting insiders out, will we or nil we, making new concatenations out of old dissimilitudes. Doesn't that express it?"

She shook her head in confusion, not sure what had been expressed. "Are you saying I shouldn't bother to wait for Plandybast?"

"Leave him a note. Tell him to meet you on the road south of Pfarb Durim tonight with any of his people who will assist or to go to Himaggery and offer himself if you are not there. In that way, you need not linger, wasting time, and it is indeed a waste. If one may not sleep and one may not act, then what use is there sitting about?''

After a moment's thought, she did as the Agirul suggested, finding a bit of flat stone on which a charcoaled message could be left. He could not fail to see it. The letters were as tall as her hand, and the Agirul assured her there would be no rain, no storm to wipe them away in the next few hours. "Where, then?" she asked him. "Back to Pfarb Durim?"

"I thought we might seek assistance from some other source,'' the Agirul replied, lapsing into shadowperson talk while the little ones gathered around in a mood of growing excitement. "I have suggested they take you to Ganver's Grave. It is not far from here, and the trip may prove helpful.''

"Ganver's Grave? We have no dead raisers among us, Agirul. And truth to tell, after Hell's Maw, I have no desire to see or smell any such.''

"Tush. The place may be called Ganver's Grave, girl, but I did not say he is dead. Go along. It is not far, but there is no time to spend in idle chat.''

"Are you coming?" she inquired, offering to help it down from the branch it hung upon.

"I'll be there," it said, humming, still swinging. "More or less.''

Shaking her head she allowed herself to be led away, following the multitude which scampered ahead of her into the trees. A tug at her hand reminded her that a small person waited to be carried, and she lifted him onto her shoulder once more. He kicked her, and she shifted, making it easier for him and herself to catch up to the fleeing shadows before them.

They led east, back toward the River, she thought, and the long valley in which it ran. The land was flat, easy to move across, with little brush or fallen wood to make the way difficult. After they had run for some little time, Mavin began to wonder at the ease of the travel and to look at the land about her with more questioning eyes. It looked like—like park land. Like the land at the edge of the p'natti, where all the dead wood had been cut for cook fires and all noxious weeds killed. It looked used, tended. "Who lives here?" she panted, receiving a warble which conveyed no meaning in answer. "Someone," she said to herself. "Something. Not shadowpeople. They would not cut brush or clear out thorns." Someone else. Something else. "Maybe some Demesne or other. Some great Gamesman's private preserve." But, if so, where were the thousand gardeners and woodsmen it would take? She had run many leagues, and the way was still carefully tended and groomed and empty. "If there are workers, where are they?"

She heard a warbling song from far ahead, one which grew louder as she ran. The shadowpeople had stopped, had perhaps arrived at their goal. She ran on, feeling the warmth of her hindquarters as the sun rolled west. There through the trees loomed a wall of color, a towering structure which became more and more visible, wider and wider, until she emerged from the trees and saw all of it, an impossibility, glowing in the light. "Ooof," she whispered, not believing it.

"Ooof," carolled the shadowpeople in sympathy, coming back to pat her with their narrow hands and bring her forward.

It was stone, she thought. Like the stone of which the strange arches were made. Although they were green and this was red as blood, both had the same crystalline feel, the misleading look of translucence. The wall bulged toward her out of the earth, then its glittering pate arched upward at the sky. "A ball," she marveled. "A huge ball, sunk a bit in the ground. What is it? Some kind of monument? A memorial? Agirul called it Ganver's Grave. Is Ganver buried here?''

"Unlikely," said the Agirul from a tree behind her. "I don't think the Eesties bury their dead. I don't think Eesties die, come to think of it. At least I never heard one of them say anything to indicate that they might. Not that I've been privileged to hear them say that much. No, I've probably not heard a word from an Eesty more than a dozen times in the last two or three thousand years.''

"You're that old! Two or three thousand years!"

The beast shifted, as though uncomfortable at her vehemence. "Only in a sense, Mavin. What the Agirul knows, the Agirul knows. It may not have been precisely 'I' who spoke with the Eesties, but then it was in a sense. The concept is somewhat confusing, I realize. It has to do with extracorporeal memory and rather depends upon what filing system one uses. None of which has any bearing on the current situation at all. We came, I believe, to seek some help, and should be getting at it.'' The Agirul came painfully out of its tree and began dragging itself toward the red ball, moving with so much effort and obvious discomfort that Mavin leaned over and picked it up, gasping at the effort. The Agirul was far heavier than its size indicated, though she was able to bear the weight once it had positioned itself upon her back. She would need more bulk if she were to bear this one far, but the creature gave her no time to seek it. "Around to the side, to your left. There's a gateway there. It will probably take all of us to get it open.''

The gateway would have taken all of them and a hundred or so more to open, had it not stood open already, a curved section a man-height thick, peeled back like the skin of a thrilp to show a dark, pointed doorway leading inside.

"You want us to go in there?" she asked. "In the dark?"

"Not we," said the Agirul. "You. Mavin. Don't worry about translation. If you meet an Eesty, you'll be able to understand him. Or her. Or thir. Or fle. Or san. Whichever. The polite form of address is 'aged one.' And the polite stance is attentive. Don't miss anything, or you may find you've missed it all. Go on now. Not much time left." It dropped from her back and gave her an enormous shove, one which propelled her to the edge of the black gateway, over which she tripped, to fall sprawling within, within, within. . . .

There was no within.

She stood on a shifting plain beside a row of columns. Upon each column rested a red ball, tiny in comparison to the great one she had entered, and translucent, for she could see shapes within, moving gently as though swayed by a quiet sea. A gravel path ran beside the column, gemmy blue and green and violet stones, smoothly raked. Mavin turned to see a small creature pick up a round stone from the side of the path, nibble at it experimentally, then nip it quickly with his teeth, faceting the stone, polishing it with a raspy black tongue before raking it to the path with its claws. It moved on to another stone, taking no notice of her. When she knelt to look at it more closely, it did not react in any way. It had no eyes that she could see, no ears, only two pale, clawed hands, a mouth like a pair of steel wedges, and two pudgy legs on which to move about. It faceted another stone, then extended its neck and its hands to roll rapidly away on its feet, its hands, and the top of its head, like a wheel, disappearing into the distance.

This drew her eyes to the horizon, a very close one, as though the ground beneath her curved more than what she was used to. On that horizon marched a line of towers, each tower topped by a red ball, in each ball a hint of movement as of something moving slightly in its sleep or a watchman shifting restlessly upon a parapet. Between these towers giant wheels were rolling, creature wheels, stopping now and then to polish one of the towers with great, soft hands or trim the grassy verge with wide, scissory teeth before rolling on like huge children turning endless handsprings. Mavin moved toward them, noticing the sound her feet made on the jeweled gravel, an abrupt, questioning sound, as of someone saying "what" over and over again. She moved to the grass, only to leap back again, for the grass screamed when she stepped upon it, a thin wailing of pain and outraged dignity. So she went on, the gravel saying "what" beneath her feet, the grass weeping at her side, each section taking up the complaint as she passed.

Flowers began to appear along the verge, gray blossoms the size of her hands, five-petaled, turning upon their stems like windmills with a shrill, determined humming. Creeping, grublike things lay upon the stems of the flowers. Mavin watched as the creepers extended long, sharp tusks into the whirling petals, cutting them into fragments which floated upon the air only an instant before opening like tiny books and flying away.

Bushes along the road began to lash their branches, each branch splitting into a bundle of narrow whips which exploded outward into a net. The nets cast almost to the road, missing her, though not by much. Some of the flower creepers were caught and dragged back toward the bushes while they plied their tusks frantically, trying to cut free. The gravel went on saying "what."

She came near to the first of the towers, stepping aside to avoid the nets, paying no more attention to the crying grass. The gravel fell silent beneath her feet, and she stood gazing upward at the ruby globe, twice her

156 Sheri S. Tepper

own height in diameter, with something moving in it.
Was this an Eesty? Was it alive? How did one attract its
attention? There was nothing in this place to tell her the
time, to tell her how many hours there might be between
now and midnight. How many of these globes dared she
knock upon, if knocking was the thing to do?

Then she remembered what Agirul had said. Remembered, stood back from the globe, and cried in a voice
which would have broken rock had any been present to
be broken, "Aged one. Oh, oho, aged one! I cry for
assistance!"

At first there was only an agitation within the globe,
as though a bubble of air had burst or some small thing
whipped around in its shadowed interior, but then lines
began to glow down the sides of it, golden lines, from
the apex down the sides, running beneath the globe
where it sat on its pillar, glowing brightly and more
brightly until she could see that they were actually lines
graven into the globe, pressing down into its mirror-
smooth surface. The lines darkened, deepened, turned
black with a sudden cracking sound as of breaking
glass. Then the sections began to fold outward, five of
them, opening like a flower's petals to the sky, crisp and
hard at first, turning soft, beginning to droop over the
pillar to disclose what sat within.

Which was a star-shaped mound, one leg drooping
over each opened petal, the center pulsating slowly as
though breathing, the whole studded with small, ivory
projections. As she watched, the thing began to draw
itself upright, one limb rising, two more pushing upright, until what faced her was a five-pointed semblance
of her own shape, two lower limbs, two upper ones with
a protrusion between them containing what might be in-
terpreted as a face. At least it had a slit in it which could
be a mouth. Or could equally well be something—anything else.

She waited. Nothing further happened. Taking a stance which she defined in her own mind as attentive, she tried once more. "Aged one. Most honorable and revered aged one. I cry for help."

The voice formed in her brain, not outside it, a whispery voice, like wind, or the slow gurgle of a stream over stones, without emphasis, constantly changing yet unchanging. "Who calls Ganver for help? Ganver who gives no help? Ganver who does not interfere?"

"I was sent," she said. "Agirul sent me." There was no response to this. She tried again. "My name is Mavin. I am a shifter girl, from the world"—she waved vaguely behind her—"out there. The Ghoul Blourbast has stolen Ganver's Bone."

There was nothing, nothing. Beyond the pillar she could see another of the little jewel cutters, or perhaps the same one, burrowing into a pile of stones at the side of a branching path. It nibbled and scurried, paying no attention to her or to the star-shaped creature which confronted her. Finally the voice shaped in her mind once more.

"What is a Ghoul?"

"A Ghoul—well, a Ghoul is a person with the Talent of dead raising. Not only that. Most Ghouls eat dead flesh. And they kidnap people and kill them. And Blourbast is particularly horrible, because it is said he fastens live people to the walls of his burrows and leaves them there forever, animating the bones. And . . ."

"Such a creature, how did it come by Ganver's Bone?"

"Proom had the Bone. Do you know Proom? No, probably not. Well, Proom is a shadowperson. It is he who had the—what would you say—the *custody* of Ganver's Bone. But someone, someone very powerful, I think perhaps some one of you, that is of the Eesties, sent Proom on a journey, and he didn't want to take the

Bone. So he put it in a safe place—an old, sacred, guarded place. But Blourbast came riding, and he didn't care whether it was sacred or not, so he took it. And the little people went to sacrifice themselves to get it back, but it didn't do any good. He won't give it back. And if he doesn't they'll all die of disease. Of ghoul-plague.'' She ran out of words, unable to go on without a response. She did not know whether the thing before her had even heard her. Again she waited. Again it was long, long before the voice formed in her head.

"It is not ghoul-plague. It is a disease of the shadow-people.

"Long before there was any such thing as Ghoul, there were shadowpeople.

"Long before Ghoul ate shadowperson flesh, shadowpeople ate shadowperson flesh. Small creatures, beasts, with such aspirations, such longing for holiness.

"Ah. Sad. So sad, such longing for holiness. So it was Ganver came to them and made them a bargain. If they would stop eating flesh, Ganver would give them a Bone, a part of Ganver, a thing to call a note from the universal song that they might sing. And holiness would follow. In time. In forever. But you say the sickness is returned."

"We call it ghoul-plague, because Ghouls get it. Some of the shadowpeople were sick, but not with the plague."

"So. Then they have kept their bargain. How long? Do you know how long ago I bargained with Proom's people?"

She tried to think. What had Agirul said, that there had been no plague among the little people for what? A thousand years? More, perhaps? "A thousand years," she said. "Since Proom's many times great-grand-father. But they still do eat meat."

"True," whispered the voice. "Their bodies require

it. But they do not eat each other. That is good. Good. Thank you for coming. I will relish this news of the shadowpeople, for it has been a thousand years or more since I have seen them.''

The petals on the pillar began to harden, to draw upward. Mavin cried out in a voice of outrage: "No. You can't go. Don't you understand, the Bone is in Blourbast's hands. The little people believe they cannot cure the illness without it.''

"They cannot,'' said the voice unemotionally. "What matter is that? If they do not eat one another, they will not become sick with it.''

"The Ghoul ate shadowpeople, the Ghoul became sick with it,'' she cried. "And he has given the sickness to my brother, a boy, only a child. And others. Others who have done nothing wrong. Innocent people . . .''

"We do not interfere,'' whispered the voice.

"You did interfere,'' she shouted, stamping her foot on the gravel so that it shrieked, kicking at the grass until it wailed beneath her feet. "You gave them the Bone in the first place. That's interference. If you hadn't given it to them, they'd all have died. Then they wouldn't have been around for Blourbast to eat, and he wouldn't have gotten sick, and Mertyn wouldn't be lying in Pfarb Durim, dying, my own brother. You did interfere!''

This time there was a long silence. One of the wheel things rolled up to the pillar, lowered itself onto four limbs and polished at the pillar with the fifth before standing up once more and rolling away. As it rolled, it made a whipping sound, like the wings of a crow, receding into the distance.

"It is hard to do good,'' the voice whispered.

"Nonsense,'' she muttered. "You have only to do it.''

"Shhhh,'' the voice hissed, sounding rather like

Agirul. "Think. Ganver heard the music of the shadow-people and saw them dying. Ganver longed to help them. Ganver gave them his Bone. Was that good? At first, perhaps. Then the Bone was stolen, the shadow-people were sacrificed, now they are in danger of their lives once more—and so is another people who were not even there when the Bone was given. If the Bone had not been given, you have said what would have happened."

"They would have died," she said, mourning. "They would all have died then."

"And their song with them. All their songs. The song of Ganver, the Song of Morning, the Song of Zanbee, the Song of Mavin Manyshaped."

"But if they die, the songs will die," she argued. "We must save them. We must save Mertyn."

"A good thing. Of course. And what evil thing will come of that? Oh, persons of the world, why do you pursue the Eesties? Have we not yet learned to do nothing, not to interfere?"

"It seems to me," she said, "if you ever interfere at all, you just have to go on. You can't just say, 'Well, it isn't my fault,' and let it go at that. It is your fault. You admitted it. And aged one or not, you've just got to do something about it."

There was a feeling of sighing, a feeling beside which any other sigh which might ever be felt was only a minor thing, a momentary discomfort. This sigh was the quint-essential sigh, the ultimate sigh, and Mavin knew it as she heard it. She had asked more than she had any right to do, and she knew that as well. Gritting her teeth, she confronted the drooping Eesty and said it again.

"It's up to you to fix it."

"Tell me," whispered the voice, "what is to be done."

So she told, for the manyeth time, what was to be done. The armies of King Frogmott assembled to confront the armies of Blourbast. Blourbast himself led beneath the monuments on the road, settled there with his immediate retinue. The ritual—whatever that might be—conducted by the shadowpeople. The cure wrought —Mavin had no idea how; presumably the Eesty did, since it was the Eesty's bone which was involved. Then, when the cure was wrought and Blourbast tried to leave, then the shifters would rise up about him from their disguise as stone and tree and earth, rise up and consume him, all but Ganver's Bone. Which would be returned to the shadowpeople. . . .

"Which will be returned to me . . ." whispered the voice. "I did not intend it to be used in these games of back and forth. I am not a bakklewheep to be used in this way, cast between players in a Game I do not choose. Oh, I have been long asleep, Mavin Manyshaped, but I know of your Game world. Tell me, if I gave you my Bone, would your people cease their Game of eating one another as Proom's people stopped their own?"

She bowed her head in shame. "I do not know, aged one. Truly I do not know."

"No," it said sadly. "You do not know. Perhaps in time. There are some of you who talk with some of us. Perhaps in time. Now I have interfered once, and my holiness is dwindled thereby. I may not take myself away from it all but must continue in the way my foolishness led me. So. We will come to your place of monuments, which is also my place of monuments—for they are my people as well—when the blue star burns in the horns of Zanbee. And later, Mavin Manyshaped, I will regret what I have done, and you must pray peace for me."

The thing came down from its pillar, all at once, so quickly that she did not see it move. It rolled, as the smaller creatures had rolled, and it made a music in its rolling, a humming series of harmonic chords which caught her up into them so that she could not tell where she was. She felt herself move, or the world move beneath her. It was impossible to tell which. There were stars overhead, and a sound of singing, and she heard Himaggery's voice crying like a mighty horn.

Chapter 9

It was dark. She could hear Himaggery shouting at someone, his voice carrying fitfully on the shifting wind which whipped her hair into her eyes. There were stars blooming above her, and Zanbee, the crescent moon, sailed upon the western edge of the sky. She searched for the blue star, finding it just below the moon. Soon it would hang upon the moon's horns, or appear to do so, and she had no idea where the hours had gone since afternoon.

She stared into the dark, making her eyes huge to take in the light, blinding herself at first on the arcing rim of fire which burned at one side until she identified it as the torches of King Frogmott's army gathered on the high rim about Pfarb Durim, between her and the city. Soon her eyes and mind began to interpret what she saw, and she located the place she stood upon, a small hill just west of the road where the Strange Monuments loomed among lights which moved and darted, hither and thither, and from which the Wizard's voice seemed to emanate.

"The Agirul says they've left the place below. It will take them almost till midnight to get here. Help the shadowpeople with that cauldron. . . ."

She couldn't see enough through the flickering lights to know what was going on. But the closer she came the more confused things became, and when she stood at Himaggery's side while he fumed over some drawing in the dust, she knew less than she had to begin with. She laid a hand upon his shoulder and was surprised to feel him leap as though he had been burned.

"Mavin," he shouted at her. "You . . . where have you . . . they said you might not . . ." Then as she was about to make soothing sounds, he said more quietly "Sorry. Things have been a bit hectic. I had word that you probably wouldn't make it back, and that you wouldn't bring any of your kin to help. Except the fellow who brought the message, of course. Your thalan, is it? Plandybast? Nice enough fellow. A bit too apologetic, but then it doesn't seem that the Battlefox branch of your family has much to recommend it outside himself, so perhaps he has aplenty to apologize for."

"Plandybast came then," she said in wonder. "I really didn't think he would." She leaned over the dirt where he had been drawing diagrams. "What are we doing? Have you changed the plan?"

"Of course. Not once or twice, but at least six times. At first we couldn't find a Herald, but then I managed to locate one I knew slightly. Subborned him, I suppose one might say, right out of Frogmott's array."

"And you sent him to Blourbast."

"To the front door. What there is of it. Most of Poffle is underground, as you well know, and what shows above ground isn't exactly prepossessing. Well, the fellow went off to Blourbast full of Heraldish dignity and made his move, cried challenge on the Ghoul to bring the amulet—that's what we decided to call it, an amulet. Why let the Ghoul know what he's holding?— to the Monuments at midnight tonight to assist in preparing a cure for the plague. We didn't let on that we know he has the disease himself. The Herald just went on about honor and Gamesmanship and all the rest.''

"Was there a reply?"

"Not at first. We thought there wasn't going to be, and I'd started to re-plan the whole thing. Then this woman came out. It must be his sister, the Harpy. . . ."

"Pantiquod."

"Right. She came out and gave us a lot of double talk which meant that Blourbast would show up but that he didn't trust us. So he would come with a retinue. That's what she called it. A retinue. By that time it was getting on evening, and Proom showed up with the Agirul. Or rather Proom showed up and we found the Agirul hanging in a tree by the side of the road. Fortuitous.''

"Fortuitous," repeated Mavin, not believing it.

"Among the three of us, we decided that 'retinue' probably means the entire army of Hell's Maw as well as a few close kin and men sworn to the Ghoul. And about that time your thalan arrived to tell us you probably wouldn't be coming if you weren't here already. You'd left him a note or something?''

"Or something, yes."

"Which meant I had to plan it again. And then Proom's been busy with his kindred. Evidently this ritual hasn't been performed for a thousand years, and there's only a song to guide them in the proper procedures, so it's been sing and run, run and sing every moment since dark. Now we've just received word that Blourbast and his retinue—we were right, it is the army —are on the road coming up from Hell's Maw. So. Now here you are.''

"I'm sorry I'm late," she said, starting to tell him

about the Eesty, wondering why the Agirul and Proom had not already done so, only to find that she could say nothing about it at all. The words stuck. She thought them clearly, but her throat and tongue simply didn't move. She did not choke or gasp or feel that she was being throttled. There was not any sense of pain, but the words would not come.

Then for the first time she wondered about the Eesty and looked around for it. Nothing. Dark and stars and the flicker of torches: shouting, fragments of song from the area around the arches, nothing more. And yet the darkness was not empty. She could feel it boiling around her, something living, running its quick tentacles through her hair, its sharp teeth along her spine. She shivered with a sharp, anticipatory hunger, a hunger for action, for resolution, a desire to make something episodic out of the tumbled events of her recent past.

"You're forgiven," he said distractedly. "Some day you must tell me all about it. But right now we've got to figure out how to accomplish everything that needs doing in this one final do."

She crouched beside his diagram. "Show me."

"King Frogmott's army is here," he said, retracing a wide circle just inside the line that was the arc of road outside Pfarb Durim. "From the cliff's edge south of the city, all along the inner edge of the road, curving around and then over to the cliff at the north side of the city. On high ground, all the way, able to see everything."

"Except a Wizard who may want to get out," she remarked in a quiet voice, not expecting the hand he raised to stroke her face.

"Except that," he agreed in a satisfied voice. "There's another line back a few leagues, one which encloses Pfarb Durim and Poffle, but those besiegers cannot see what is going on. Now, the road which comes up from Poffle to the top of the cliff is *outside* Frogmott's lines, so Blourbast can bring his ghoulish multitude up and along toward the Monuments. The Agirul and I believe he will marshall his own army in a long array between him and King Frogmott's men. He will want to be protected against the besiegers, for they have threatened anyone who comes out carrying the plague. Then, having protected himself against King Frogmott, he will bring a considerable group with him to the Monuments—to protect himself against whoever is here. The Herald challenged him in my name. Huld may have mentioned me to him. I don't know who else he expects to find here, but he certainly won't come alone.''

"I was supposed to shift . . . where he'd be."

"You were supposed to shift. Right. You and a dozen more just like you. Well, two of you just aren't enough, that's all. I had hoped we could make a very natural-looking setting, one he wouldn't hesitate to sit himself down in comfortably, but with only two of you, what could we manage? A couple of rocks, trees?"

"I've never tried a tree," she said in a small voice. "Or a rock either. I haven't had much time for practice."

"Rocks aren't easy," said a voice from behind them. "I hate to do them myself. Trees are easier, but they do take practice. I could probably show Mavin how in an hour or so. . . ."

"Plandybast." She turned to him gladly. "I didn't think you'd come. I really didn't. I thought Itter would talk you out of it."

"Itter is always perfectly logical," said Plandybast, rather sadly. "But she's frequently wrong, and after a while I just get very tired of listening to her. The others haven't been disillusioned, not yet, but the time will come. Until then I'll just have to do what I think is right and let her fuss if she wishes. And she will."

"What are the shadowpeople doing?" she asked. "Is it anything we could help with?"

"I think not," said Himaggery. "They located an ancient cairn near the road and moved it to disclose a huge old cauldron underneath. They rolled that over to the middle of the road under the arches, dragged in a huge pile of wood for a fire, and now they're out on the hills gathering herbs and blossoms and who knows what. Meantime they've assembled an orchestra all over the hills—I have never seen so many drums in my life—and what seems to be the greater part of several other tribes. For a creature that I have always considered to be mythical, it seems to be extremely numerous."

"I doubt we'd ever have seen them in the ordinary way of life," Mavin said. "If it hadn't been for Blourbast and the plague."

"And Mertyn," he said, touching her face again. "And Mavin."

She flushed and turned away toward the dark to hide it. She wanted, didn't want him to touch her again; wanted, didn't want him to look at her in that particularly half-hungry fashion; wanted, didn't want the time to wear on and things to happen which would take him from her side and throw them both into violent, unthinking action. "Why should I feel safer fighting Ghouls," she asked herself, rhetorically, not seeking an answer, not wanting an answer.

"You'll have to give me something to do," she said. "I can't have run all this way just to sit and do nothing."

He sighed, looked for a moment older than his years as the firelight flickered across his face. She could imagine him as he would be at age forty, tall, strong, but with the lines deep between his eyes and at the sides of his mouth, lines of both laughter and concentration. And some of anger, she told herself. Some of anger, too. He said, "Whenever Blourbast and his crew get themselves settled, try to get close to him, as close as you can. Then when the cure is done or made or created, if you can do it without getting hurt—remember, there are no Healers closer than Betand—if you can do it without getting hurt, try to get the Bone. Then get away from him."

"You don't want us to try to dispatch him?" asked Plandybast.

"If there were a dozen of you, yes. With two of you, no. Just get the Bone and get out. The dispatching of Blourbast will have to wait for another time."

They sat, the three of them, staring down at the lines in the dirt, the curving arc of the road, the waving line of the cliff's edge, the x's marking the army of the King. The Strange Monuments loomed beside them, and on the road the shadowpeople scampered and sang to one another, short bursts of music which sounded harsh and dissonant.

"One of Proom's people says the Ghoul is almost at the cliff's top," said the Agirul from behind them. Mavin had not known it was there, and she tried to see it, but saw only the massed bulk of foliage against the lighter sky.

"Who does he have with him?" asked the Fon.

"In addition to the army, there is his sister and her twins, Huld and Huldra. Then there are a few guards, a Sorcerer, two Armigers, two Tragamors."

"And here, with us?"

"Me," said Himaggery. "And you two shifters. Proom and his people. The Agirul. And my friend the Herald. He is waiting in the trees to make whatever announcements may seem most useful."

"Windlow?" she asked. "Mertyn?"

"I haven't been back in the city," he said softly. "I don't know, Mavin. Believe me, Windlow will have done everything possible for him."

"I know," she admitted. "Except that it is hard to let someone else do it while I am out here, not knowing."

"We'd better get out of the light," he said. "I'll go down near the road. We found some logs to use as seats for Blourbast, arranged where we want him, in the middle of the road. We'll try to get him there. Once he is there, do what you can. . . ."

He left the two shifters, taking the torch with him. They sat for a moment silent, then Mavin said, "A log should be easier than a tree."

"It is," Plandybast admitted. "Much."

"We couldn't be much closer than to have him sitting on us."

"If the small ones do not make the cure . . ." Plandybast said, "and he is sitting on us . . ."

"They'll make it. Plandybast, I've seen them do wonderful things. Don't doubt it for a moment." And she drew him up to follow her down into the darkness of the road where the shadowpeople had lighted the fire beneath their cauldron and a pungent smoke poured into the night sky, making her dizzy yet at the same time less troubled. It was not difficult to become a log. She shifted once or twice, then simply lay there and let the smoke wreath her around, driven as it was by a downdraft of the fitful wind.

She heard Huld's voice first, a petulant whine, a sneering tone, "They have made a place for you, dear thalan. The seats are not what you are accustomed to, I fear. There is no velvet cushion."

"Hush, dear boy. I have no need for velvet cushions. Does one need a velvet cushion to witness a wonder? Hmmm? And are we not to witness a wonder tonight? The making of a plague cure? Who has heard of such a thing? The Healers will be frantic with embarrassment and envy. Not a bad thing, either. I am not fond of Healers."

Another voice, so like Huld's that it might have been mistaken for his, yet higher, lighter. "Dear brother, dear thalan, indeed we would all dispense with cushions to see this thing. And to take—what may I say?— advantage of it."

"Be silent, girl," said Pantiquod, following them down onto the road where they clustered around the logs with their guardsmen, all staring suspiciously into the darkness. "Say nothing you would not like to have overheard. The dark is all around us, and it trembles with ears."

"Of course, mother," said the voice sweetly. "One would not wish to be overheard saying that a cure of the plague is of great interest to us."

"Your mother said hush," grated the Ghoul. "Now I say to you hush, Huldra. You may think that child in you protects you from my displeasure, but I have no care for that. If you trouble me, girl, both you and the child may go into hell for all me."

"Not so quick, thalan," purred Huld. "I am thalan to the child in her womb, you know. Mine own. And mine own child, too—as is the teaching of the High King, away there in the south—a child linked to me doubly if not to you at all. So, Blourbast, go quietly with my gentle sister or I will make your sickness seem a day's walk in the sun."

"Let us all be still," said Pantiquod. "We are here for a reason. Let the reason be manifest. I see nothing except fitful torches and scampering shadows. Is this a mockery?"

"No mockery, madam," came Himaggery's voice from the dark. "The blue star moves toward the horns of Zanbee. The little people of the forests have lit their fires beneath the great cauldron. They will begin to sing soon. There will be drums, voices, manifestations. At some point in the ritual, I will call to you to strike the . . . amulet you carry. Strike it then, and the cure will be made.

"I will return in time. Until then, seat yourselves and do not disrupt what must occur." They heard him moving away into the shadows.

"Where will this cure be made?" asked Huldra, seating herself on Mavin's back with a moue of discontent. "What form will it take?"

"They have spoken of a cauldron," said the Harpy Pantiquod. "Undoubtedly the cure will be therein. When it is made, we must move quickly to take it. If the cauldron is too heavy to be carried, then we will take what we can in our flasks and dump the rest upon the ground."

"How dreadful for Pfarb Durim," said Huld. "They will not receive their portion."

"I have promised you Pfarb Durim," said the Ghoul. "When it is empty."

"I am glad you remember that promise," said Huld, fingering the dagger at his side. "It is a promise I hope much upon. There are some in that city who may not die of plague, and I wish to be first among them like a fustigar among the bunwits. They have not pleased me."

"Did the old Seer speak nastily to my dear brother?" the woman beside him drawled. "Did the little Wizard make him unhappy?"

"Be still, girl. There are things I could do to you which would not affect the child, so do not count too much upon my forbearance. Hush. What is that?"

The sound was of many drums throughout the hills near the road, drum heads roaring to the tumbling thump of a thousand little hands, like soft thunder far among mountains. Flutes came then, softly, a dawn

birdsong of flutes, then gentle bells, music to wake one
who had slept a long sleep.

The fire beneath the cauldron blazed up, and they
could see the tiny shadows which crossed before it,
black against the amber light, some dragging more
wood to the fire, others tossing their burdens into the
cauldron. Steam rose from the cauldron to join the
smoke of the fire, and this moist, woodsy mist waved
back and forth across the road, wreathing the bases of
the Monuments, seeming to soak into the crystalline
material of which they were made, making them appear
soft and porous. One could almost see the mists sucked
up into them, the softness moving upward on each arch,
out of the firelight into the high darkness.

The smell of the mist reached them at the same time
the voices began to sing, taking up the bell song and re-
peating it, close, far, close again, first the highest voices
and then the deeper, again and again. A lone trumpet
began to ride high upon the song, higher yet, impossibly
treble above the singing, while some bass horn or some
great stone windpipe blew notes almost below their
hearing so that the ground trembled with it.

The earth trembled, trembled, then moaned.

Beside them the base of the Strange Monument
shivered in the earth. The pedestal beneath it shifted,
groaned, and then was still.

Mavin created eyes in the top of her log shape and
looked up. The arch was glowing green: diagonally
across the width of it a dark line appeared, deeper with
each moment. Then the sound of breaking glass cracked
through the music and the top of the arch split in two
lengthwise, each part coiling upward like a serpent to
stand high above its base, each arch becoming two
tapered pillars which waved in the music like reeds in
wind.

The watchers shivered. The Monuments danced,

reaching toward one another across the road, beside the road, bowing and touching their tips, two great rows of tapered towers, dancing green in the night as the drums went on and on and the mists from the cauldron rose more thickly upon the shifting wind.

"Keep your eyes on that cauldron," hissed the Ghoul. "Move to capture it as soon as I strike the amulet." The men behind him murmured assent even as they shifted uneasily, feeling the earth teeter beneath them.

Now the contents of the cauldron began to glow, a pillar of ruby light rising out of the vessel toward the zenith. The singers had moved closer to the road, their voices rising now in an almost unbearable crescendo. Mavin held herself rigid, though she wanted to weep, faint, curl up where she lay into as tiny a space as she could. She heard the voice of Himaggery calling from the sidelines. "Be ready, Blourbast."

Then all that had gone before faded in a hurricane of sound, a storm of music, a shattering climax in which there were sounds of organs and trumpets and bells so huge that the world shivered. "Now, Blourbast!" came Himaggery's voice, barely audible over the tumult, and the Ghoul held up the amulet and struck it with his dagger.

One sound.

One sound, piercing sweet in silence.

Tumult over, singing over, all the terrible riot of drum and trumpet over, and only that one sound singing on and on and on into the quiet of night. The cauldron blazed up in response, the red light pouring out to spread like an ointment across the sky, into every face, onto every surface, high and low, hidden or visible, like water which could run everywhere, over the drawn battle lines of the armies, over the walls of Pfarb Durim, onto every roof, down every chimney, into every window and door, closed or open, through every wall. Only Mavin heard the *whip, whip, whip* as of great wings and only Mavin saw the huge, cloudy wheel flick through their midst in an instant, taking Ganver's Bone with it and leaving the Ghoul standing, his mouth open, his hands empty except for the dagger he had used to strike that note.

And Mavin knew why the Eesty had taken its Bone back again. It would not have done to leave that note in the hands of Gamesmen. Among the shadowpeople, perhaps, for they were attempting to be holy, though they failed from time to time, but not among the Gamesmen.

In the silent flicker of the distant fire, they saw the shadowpeople tip the cauldron over and let it empty itself on the roadway.

The Ghoul roared, spitting curses. From the roadside, Himaggery said, "You need not threaten and bluster, Ghoul. The bargain was kept. You are cured."

And Huld's voice, hissing with a scarce concealed fury, "And are those in Pfarb Durim cured as well?"

"All," said Himaggery. "All within reach of the light, and it spread as far as my eyes could see."

Huld turned on the Ghoul, dagger flicking in his hand, "Then you have not kept your promise, thalan. You have undone what you promised me."

"But, but . . ." blustered the Ghoul, the only words he had time to say, for the dagger stood full in his throat and the blood rushed behind it in a flood, soaking his chest and belly, spurting upon those who sat near him so that they recoiled, Mavin recoiled, becoming herself near the place that Himaggery stood, both to stand with shocked eyes while Huld drew his dagger out again and turned toward Himaggery with madness in his eyes.

"Your fault, Wizard. You tempted him with this cure. Pfarb Durim would have been mine except for you." And he came rushing toward Himaggery, dagger high, and Himaggery with no protection at all—

Save Mavin, before him, furious, suddenly taking the shape of another Gamesman, without thinking, without planning, so it was Blourbast stood before Huld's onrush and roared into his face like some mighty beast with such ferocious aspect and horrible, bleeding gash of throat that Huld stopped, eyes glazed, screamed, and turned to stumble away into the night. The others, also, Pantiquod and Huldra and the guardsmen, frantic, overwrought, driven half mad by the music and then fully mad to see Blourbast's body stand before them again.

The shape dropped away. Mavin found herself standing bare in the roadway, covered with Blourbast's blood, too weary to shift a covering for herself. She felt Himaggery's cloak swing around her, his arms draw her close. A quavering voice asked, "Is it all right to change now?" and Himaggery replied,

"Yes, Plandybast. It's all over. You can unlog yourself."

"I'm glad there wasn't any real violence," said Plandybast. "I've never been able to handle violence."

"I'm glad, too," said Himaggery, lifting her up and carrying her away to the comfortable shelter of the trees.

"Is she all right?" asked the Agirul.

"She's covered with blood," said Himaggery. "See if you can get someone to bring water." Then he sat beneath the tree, cuddling her close in his arms. She could not remember being so held, not ever, not even by Handbright in the long ago. She sighed, a sigh very like the Eesty's sigh, and let all of it fade away into dark.

Chapter 10

When morning came, they went into Pfarb Durim. The armies of King Frogmott were no barrier. The sickness had been spreading among the besiegers, and the cure was as evident to them as it was to those in the city. Indeed, when Mavin and Himaggery passed, they were already taking down the tents and putting out the fires, preparatory to the long march back to the marshes of the upper Graywater, to the northeast.

They found Mertyn still in the room in which they had left him, Windlow still by his side, though both were sound asleep on the same bed, and Himaggery forebore to wake them. Instead, he ordered a room for Mavin, and a bathtub, and various wares from clothiers and makers of unguents. By the time Mertyn wakened, she was more mistress of herself than she had ever been in Danderbat keep or since.

All of this had gone to make her a little shy, not least by the fact that she knew things the others did not, and could not tell them. She had been unable to speak of them even to the Agirul when she had wakened beneath his tree that morning. She had tried, and the Agirul had opened one slitlike eye to peer at her as though it had never seen her before and would not see her again.

"Many of us," it said·at last, "remember things that cannot be shared. Sometimes we remember things that did not really happen. Does that make them less true? An interesting philosophical point which you may enjoy thinking about at odd times." Then it had gone back to sleep, and she had given up. She did not for one moment believe that she remembered a thing which had not happened, but she was realist enough to know that it would be her own story, her own memory, and only that.

Now she sat at Mertyn's side in her luxurious room— he had been moved as soon as he woke—looking out across the cliff edge to the far west. "Schlaizy Noithn is there," she said to him. "Southwest, there beyond the firehills. Perhaps Handbright is there."

"There was more to her leaving Danderbat keep than you told me, wasn't there?" He was still pale and weak from not having eaten for some days, but his eyes were alert and sparkling. "Are you going to tell me?"

"Perhaps someday," she said. "Not now."

"That Wizard is in love with you," he said. "I can tell. Besides, he was talking to Windlow about it."

She didn't answer, merely sat looking at the horizon. The sea was there, beyond the firehills. She wondered if she could find her way back to Ganver's Grave. She wondered if Ganver's Grave had not been moved elsewhere.

"He'll probably ask you to go with them."

"Where are they going?"

"Windlow has a school at the High Demesne, near the Lakes of Tarnoch. That's far to the south, west of Lake Yost."

"That's right," she mused. "Valdon is the King's

son. And Boldery. Windlow is to educate them both."

"Not Valdon," Mertyn went on, a little cocky, as though he had had something to do with it. "Valdon and that Huld got along so well that Windlow had words with Valdon about it, and that made Valdon mad, so he took the servants and went riding out at dawn. He says Windlow may school Boldery all he likes, but Valdon will have none of it."

"That's too bad," she said. "If he follows Huld, it will be the death of him." She turned to find the boy's eyes fixed on her in wonder.

"That's what Windlow says. He had a vision about it," he said.

"It doesn't take a vision. Anyone would know. Huld is walking death to anyone who comes near him. Well, he's gone, for a time at least."

"And the plague is cured. And Windlow says so long as no one eats shadowpeople—yech, I wouldn't—no one will ever get the plague again. You don't think anyone ever will, do you?"

She shrugged. "Many strange things happen, Mertyn, brother boy."

There was a light knock on the door. She opened it to let Windlow and the Fon come in, Boldery close behind them bearing a wrapped gift.

"I brought it for Mertyn," he said. "Really, it's for us both." Then, "It's a game," he announced proudly to Mertyn. "I came to play it with you."

"The Seer and I thought—that is, we felt the boys might like to play together for a time while we have a meal downstairs." The Fon held out his hand to her, but she only smiled at him, using her own hands to gather her skirts. They had not been much for skirts at Danderbat keep. She rather liked the feel, the luxurious sway of the heavy material at her ankles and the warmth around her legs, but they still took a bit of managing.

"I'd like that." She smiled at them both, going out the door and preceding them down the stairs. There was a table set for them on a paved terrace beside a fountain, and the servants of the Mont were busy in attendance. There was fruit and wine already on the table. She sat and stared at it, smiling faintly, not seeing it.

"Mavin." She did not reply. "Mavin, what are you thinking about? Are you troubled by the Ghoul's death?" She looked up to find Windlow's eyes fixed on her, his face full of concern.

Briskly she shook her head, clearing it, giving up the dreamy fog she had moved in since waking. "I'm sorry, Seer," she said. "Today has been . . . today has been like a dream. It is hard to wake up."

"It's the first time in days you have not had to do something outrageous," he replied, spooning thrilp slices into his mouth. "Quite frankly, it's the first such day for me, too, in a very long while. Prince Valdon was not an easy traveling companion. Huld was worse, of course, but not by much. I understand he made off into the woods?"

"No doubt he is back in Poffle by now," she said. "His sister is pregnant. By him, he says. Their mother the Harpy is with them. I would say Huld is master in Hell's Maw now."

"I had hoped the place was empty."

"Not now, not soon," she said. "Though it is bound to come, one day."

"Aha," he laughed. "So now you are a Seer."

"No." She frowned. "Now I am beginning to learn to use my brain." She laughed in return. "It is like Seeing in one way. It, also, can be wrong from time to time."

The Fon sat while they talked, watching her hungrily, eating little. When the waiters had brought fresh bread and bits of grilled sausage, he said, "Mavin, will you be going to Battlefox keep, now that you have been there once and seen the people?"

"No. No, our thalan, Plandybast, is a good fellow, as you yourself said, Fon. But that is not what I want for Mertyn. Mertyn has Talent, you know. Beguilement. He has had it since he was a fifteen-season child. It is a large Talent, and he must learn to manage it. They could do nothing for him in Battlefox save savage him and make him vicious with it. No. He must have a good teacher." She was looking at Windlow as she said it, half smiling. "I spoke with him about it, and he told me what teacher he would prefer. Of course, I cannot pay much in the way of fees."

"I will pay the fees," choked the Fon. "In return for saving my life, Mavin. Huld would have killed me."

"He would have tried. I think you might have stopped him quite successfully."

"And you, Mavin?" asked Windlow, quietly, softly, like a child trying to capture a wild bunwit without scaring it. "You?"

"Will you come with Mertyn?" The Fon, less wary, too eager.

"No," she said.

"No? Never?"

She shook her head, biting her lip over an expression which might have been part smile. "I did not say never. I only said no, I will not come with Mertyn." She folded her napkin as she had seen other diners do, reached out to take their hands, one on each side.

"I am Mavin of Danderbat keep? What is a Mavin of Danderbat keep? What shape is it? What color is it? What does it feel and know in its bones? Does it fly? Crawl? Does it grow feathers or fur?

"What places has it seen? What Assemblies has it attended? You who are not shifters do not know what an assembly is, and neither really does a shifter girl who has not left her keep to go into the wide world.

"What is in Schlaizy Noithn? For me?

"No, Fon. I will not come with Mertyn now. Though I may, some day. Some day."

And she would not let them try to dissuade her, nor would she let the Fon be near her with the two of them alone, for she knew what her blood would do and how little her head could manage it. Instead, a day or two later, she stood beside the parapet with him, with Boldery and Mertyn playing at wands and rings nearby, and told him farewell.

"My sister is out there somewhere. I would like to find her, see if I can help her. She may need my help. As for you, Fon, you do not need my help, not now."

"Do not call me Fon. You named me before. I am the Wizard Himaggery, and I will be that Wizard until you name me else."

"The Fon is dead." She laughed shakily. "Long live the Himaggery."

"So be it." He was not laughing at all. "Will you make a bargain with me, Mavin?"

"What sort of bargain?"

"If you go out into the world, and if the world is exciting, and you forget me, and time spins as time does, and the world passes as the world does, will you return to this place twenty years from now and meet me here if you have not seen me before then?"

"Twenty years? So long? Do you think I will not seek my friends out long before that?"

"Well, and if you do, better yet. But will you promise me, Mavin?"

"I'll be old, wrinkled."

"It will not matter. Will you promise me?"

"Oh, that I'll promise!" She laughed up into his unlaughing face.

"On your honor?"

"On my honor. On my Talent. On my word."

"Twenty years?"

"Twenty years." She turned away, biting her lip, afraid that her calm might break and the tears spill over. "Now. I am going west, my friend. I have made my farewells to Mertyn." She reached out to stroke his face as he had done so many times to hers, then turned down the stairs and away down the street of the city, without looking back.

Windlow came to him where he stood, looking after her. "Did she make the promise?"

"Yes."

"Did she know it was a Seeing of mine?"

"I didn't tell her."

"Does she know she will not see you again until then?"

"I didn't tell her," he said. "I could not bear to say it. I can not bear to think of it now."

The road south of Pfarb Durim is arched by great, strange monuments. Mavin Manyshaped walked that way, seeing the arches with new eyes. She felt eyes from the branches of the trees watching her pass. On the hills, voices added to a song, spinning it into a lazy chant which made small echoes off the Strange Monuments, almost like an answer.

As for her, her eyes were fixed on the horizon where Schlaizy Noithn lay, and the western sea. There was something in her mind of wings. And something of places no other eyes than hers had ever seen. "I am the servant of the Wizard Himaggery," she sang, quoting the Mavin of a younger time. "Perhaps," she sang, making a joyful shout at the sky. "But not yet!"

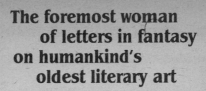